THE BUY BACK BLUES

Also by Ralph Dennis

The War Heist

The Hardman Series

Atlanta Deathwatch
The Charleston Knife is Back in Town
The Golden Girl And All
Pimp For The Dead
Down Among The Jocks
Murder Is Not An Odd Job
Working For The Man
The Deadly Cotton Heart
The One Dollar Rip-Off
Hump's First Case
The Last Of The Armageddon Wars
The Buy Back Blues

THE BUY BACK BLUES

RALPH DENNIS

ISBN: 1941298532
ISBN-13: 978-1-941298-53-4

Published by
Brash Books, LLC
12120 State Line #253
Leawood, Kansas 66209
www.brash-books.com

PUBLISHER'S NOTE

This book was originally published in 1977 and reflects the cultural and sexual attitudes, language, and politics of the period.

CHAPTER ONE

I don't know Barbara very well.

I suppose that's because when I see her, I'm always seated at one of the tables in her section. I'm always ordering another drink and she's sprinting away for it. And I see about as much of her back as her front.

If I had to guess her age, I'd put it somewhere near thirty-five. The waitress outfit, black with a little white apron, makes her seem shorter than she really is. She might be five-four or five. Her hair is cut short and it's always neat and the streaks of gray in it look real, like she's earned them.

Beyond that I don't know much about her. She's pleasant enough and she tries hard to get the right dressing on the right salad and I guess I tip her a bit more than I do the other waitresses at Mame's Bar and Grill. Maybe that's because there's a childlike quality to her, that she's lost or about to lose her way.

It was the kind of morning when I thought about moving away from Atlanta. Each summer. In late July and August, the temperature is eighty by ten in the morning and after that it's only a matter of how high it will go. All around town you hear the spit-spat noise that air conditioners make when the humidity is high.

It was the first part of August and it hadn't rained in more than two weeks. The ground on all sides of my house was parched dustbowl dry. Every other day or so I'd go out after dark and water the plants, the shrubs and the bushes. At the back of the house, near the kitchen, the figs on that runt tree had stopped growing when they were about the size of green peas. The garden hose wouldn't reach that far.

It was almost ten in the morning when I got out of bed. I went out the front door, wearing my sleep-stinking t-shirt with bare feet showing under rolled up trousers, and found Barbara sitting on my front steps. My morning paper was on the step next to her hip and there were five or six stomped out cigarette butts on the bottom step next to her feet.

"I didn't want to wake you, Mr. Hardman," she said. "I saw you hadn't got your paper yet."

I took the paper when she handed it to me. I nodded her inside. "You stand another cup of coffee?"

She said that she could.

She followed me into the house. When she passed me at the kitchen stove, I saw that the cigarette butts were in the palm of her right hand. She dropped those into the trash can and took a seat at the kitchen table. I got the flame going under the water kettle and then I went over and opened the back door, the one that leads to the screened-in porch. While I was in the doorway, I checked to make sure that the porch door was closed. It was getting close to time for the wasps to start looking for places to build their winter homes. I didn't want them to choose my porch.

I felt a stir of breeze and then I excused myself and went into the bedroom and washed up and put on a clean shirt and some shoes and socks. When I returned to the kitchen, she was making the instant coffee. I took my cup and sat down at the table across from her.

"I guess I should have called, Mr. Hardman."

"Call me Jim," I said. "And it doesn't matter that much." I waited. It was her turn.

"Billy Harper said I could talk to you."

Billy Harper is a newspaper man. A lush. A good old boy drunk. I don't think I've ever seen him without a buzz of some kind on and I don't know how he keeps his job with *The Journal* unless he knows where all the important bodies are buried.

I nodded. "People talk to me all the time."

"No, he meant that I could talk to you and even if you couldn't help me it would still be between us. That you wouldn't tell anybody."

"I think that's a fair statement."

"It's about Bob."

I must have had a blank look on my face.

"My husband, Bob."

"I don't think I ever met him," I said.

"I guess you haven't." I could see that it was hard on her. First of all, she really didn't know me and now she wanted to talk about her husband and I didn't know him. But she had a good supply of guts. Head back, her back straight. "My husband, Bob ... he disappeared."

"When?"

"Friday night."

I counted back. It was the space of a long weekend. It was Tuesday now. He'd been gone about three or four days. Enough time for some young woman to wear him down and send him home. If that was what it was.

"I have to ask this, Barbara. Do you think there might be some other woman involved?"

"I don't know. I don't think so."

"This happen before?"

She shook her head. No.

"What does Bob do for a living?"

"He was in construction. That was before the business went bad. For more than a year he's been working as a bartender."

"Where?"

"Two or three places. The last place was The Captain's Bar on Courtland."

I had a sip of the coffee. My stomach made a rumble. I coughed to cover it. "How long has he been unemployed?" That was my guess. The out-of-work blues got to a man and he caught a bus going somewhere else.

"He wasn't. He's been working as a relief bartender and he's been working private parties once or twice a week."

I nodded and pushed back my chair. I went to the refrigerator. The apple juice pitcher was on the top shelf. One sniff of it and I poured it into the sink. Sour. I rinsed the pitcher and left it in the sink. "When's the last time you saw him?"

"Friday afternoon about five. He stopped by Mame's for a Coke during the cocktail hour."

That was Mame's Bar and Grill. They only served one meal a day, lunch, and then they sold booze until about eight and closed. A lot of the downtown places did that. "Anything special about him dropping by?"

She shook her head. "It was just to tell me he was working a party and wouldn't be home until late."

"You know where the party was?"

"Red would know."

"Red?"

"He's the bartender at The Captain's Bar. He has a bar help service on the side."

"A catering service?"

"It's something like that," she said. "But it's just the bar part. Red'll set up your bar or he'll furnish the booze and the bartender for one price. All a person would have to tell him is how many people are expected at the party."

"I see." It was a new business to me. I returned to the refrigerator and got a carton of eggs and a package of bacon. "Had your breakfast yet?"

"Hours ago," she said.

I threw four strips of bacon into the skillet and started it hissing at me. "Mame send you to me?"

"Billy Harper," she said.

That was right. She'd said that. "What did Billy think I could do?"

"Find Bob," she said.

"It's hard to find somebody if they don't want to be found." I watched her face. That same lost quality reached out to me. It would be hard to be rough with her.

"I don't have much money." She made a move toward her purse.

I turned away and, using the fork, I separated the strips of bacon and spread them about the skillet. When I turned back again, she had a fan of money in her hand. It was fives and tens and a twenty or two.

"Is a hundred enough?"

"For a couple of days," I said.

"I hope it doesn't take more than two days then," she said.

"Two days and I ought to know if it's worth taking it any farther." I turned the bacon and put the fork aside.

She placed the money on the table and stood. "It's almost time for me to be at work."

I followed her to the front door. This time I looked past her and saw the blue Mustang with the battered front fender and the hood about to fly away. The Mustang had been in a bad crash some time back.

Barbara stopped at the bottom step. "I'm so worried, Mr. Hardman."

"I'll see what I can do."

"If you need more money maybe I can borrow some."

"We'll worry about that later," I said. It was a kindly statement but it wasn't good business.

I stood in the doorway while she backed out of my drive. The rear springs on the Mustang made a noise like a cageful of birds.

As soon as the car went out of sight I made a run for the bacon before it burned.

✤ ✤ ✤

At noon, I buzzed Hump's apartment until he came down and swung the door open. "What's wrong, Jim? Your phone out of order?"

"Just passing by."

He looked up the stairs. "You didn't pick a good day."

"Busy?" I followed him into the hallway.

"I was." He led the way. "Come on up."

It was cool in the hall and the stairwell. And when we were in the apartment, I could feel the air conditioning drying the sweat drops that ran down the back of my neck. It was already ninety outside.

The bedroom door was open. I could hear the shower running in the bathroom. Hump edged away from me and pulled the bedroom door closed. I grinned at him. "You left your shower on."

"Not me," he said. "This Girl Scout dropped by and offered me a box of cookies if I'd let her use my shower."

"Afraid of heat stroke, huh?"

"Something like that." He sat on the end of the sofa near the bedroom door. I passed him and sat on the other side of him. Hump reached for his pack of smokes. They were on the coffee table. He shook the pack and pushed a finger into it. He mashed the pack flat. "I'm out."

I passed him mine. He lit one. I got the pack back. "I haven't seen you for a few days."

Hump blew the smoke at me. "We got work?"

"A small thing. A missing husband. Nothing in it." I ran it by for him. He knew Barbara. Like me, he didn't know much about her except that she seemed like a nice woman.

Neither of us is licensed for the work. When we worked, we called it favors. I'd been with the Atlanta cops for a few years until I got a stain on me and had to leave. One step ahead of the headhunters, the moral ones who'd wanted my hide.

I'm pudgy and overweight and I look a little older than my real age. And I'm white and balding.

Hump's my dark shadow. He's six-six or seven and he weighs on the order of 270 or so and he's black as midnight. He used to be a damned good defensive end at Cleveland until he tore up a knee and the operation didn't kiss it and make it good again.

It's a strange partnership. Neither of us wants to do more than we have to to make a living. The bare minimum. Just enough to break a sweat and pay the bills we can't dodge. The hundred dollars from Barbara wasn't more than drinks and meals for the two days of hunt. It was, I guess, what you could call a favor favor.

I realized that the shower wasn't running anymore. "You short, Hump?"

A brief shake of his head. "I've got a few hundred but I wouldn't be against a score of some kind."

"This ain't it," I said.

He agreed. "It sounds nickels and dimes."

"And not as entertaining as Girl Scouts?"

The bedroom door swung inward, open, and a tall black girl with skin the color of sourwood honey danced through the doorway and into the living room. The dance was a kind of comic ballet. All of her skin was showing and she hadn't dried any part of it. In the dance whirl, like basic training when you learn to spot aircraft from split second glimpses of them, I put together the apple-hard breasts, the slim muscular rump and the soaked pubic hair. The drops of water spotted the floor and the walls as it flew from the ends of her hair when she snapped her head.

She didn't see me. Maybe that was because she was turning too fast or it might have been because she'd closed her eyes to make sure she wouldn't get dizzy. It was when she stopped and lifted her arms, like she was expecting applause, that her eyes clicked past Hump and locked on me. I leaned forward and smiled. I saw the shock and surprise but she didn't scream. She said, "God damn you, Hump," and marched toward the bedroom.

"I'd known you'd do this I'd have sold tickets," Hump said.

The bedroom door slammed.

"That's a Girl Scout?"

"It's hard to prove," Hump said, "when she's not wearing her uniform."

"I'm convinced." I stood. "I'll leave you to your recreation."

"Where'll you be?"

"Captain's Bar on Courtland."

Hump got to his feet and looked toward the bedroom. "Meet you there in half an hour. I've got a bad back."

"That explains it."

I laughed most of the drive downtown. Giggling to myself, looking for all the world like a madman.

Courtland is the Atlanta street that has about half the hotels in town on it. A couple of them are new, just opened in the last year or two. It's a strip of restaurants, bars and hotels and that's all.

The International Motel was built some years back, before Atlanta geared itself to become the nation's best convention city. After that decision, all the new constructions were hotels, 1,000 rooms and high up and with fancy fronts and eight restaurants and bars in each of them.

The International looks like a hotel. I haven't figured why they haven't changed the sign. Maybe they've got a hundred years of paper with Motel on the letterhead that they're trying to use up.

The Captain's Bar is on the ground level, to the right of the International's lobby. There's not much lunch business, not the walk-in kind, now that the new Hilton has opened down the street. The Hilton does a fancy buffet for about two dollars. It's supposed to be a good deal, though I understand they've taken the crab salad off the salad counter.

The bar was dark and cool. There were a couple of business executive types at the other end of the bar. All dressed up and lying to each other in every possible way. I stopped at the other end of the bar, away from them. Overhearing them, all that talk about the economy, could ruin my day.

The bartender moved down the bar toward me. He was going to flesh now, but he'd been a bruiser in his good time. I figured he was about fifty now. His red hair had some gray in it and there was thick hair on his arms and on the backs of his hands. That hair was like frayed copper wire.

I ordered a draft. He drew it and rang the ticket on the register on the way back to me. He placed the beer on a coaster and dropped the ticket next to it. He was turning away when I said, "You're Red, aren't you?"

"Some people call me that." He hadn't moved but he drew back into himself, like he thought I might be a bill collector.

"Jim Hardman," I said.

The name meant nothing to him. He bounced off his eyes. "I do something for you?"

"You know Barbara, the waitress at Mame's?"

"I know her."

I had a taste of the beer while he waited. "She's missing a husband."

"Bob?"

I nodded. That sounded like the right name. "He didn't come home after he worked that party Friday night."

"That right?"

"That's right."

A tap on the bar where the two business types were. Red went down to mix them another round of martinis. He was mixing the drinks but his head was down and I had the feeling that he was thinking more about me than the drinks. It turned out that way. He put olives in both drinks and got a rank bitch from the tycoon who'd ordered a lemon twist in his.

I sipped my draft. Red didn't seem in a hurry to come back down the bar. He fished the olive from one of the drinks and added a lemon twist and then he played around the wash sink. From the business he didn't have, I assumed that he rewashed some clean glasses. I had the last swallow from my glass and pushed it toward the shallow trough at the back side of the bar. It brought him back to me.

"Barbara asked me to look for him."

"That what you want from me?"

"That's it," I said.

"I don't know where Bob is." Red placed the fresh draft in front of me.

"The party he worked Friday night … that job come through your outfit?"

"Yes."

"He work the party?"

"No complaint I know of," Red said. "In fact, I got the check that paid for the job in the mail this morning. I've been wondering why Bob didn't come by for his cut of it. If Bob's off with some dolly, that would explain it."

"That the way you figure it?"

"Nothing else it could be. Nobody's going to hold him for ransom."

"Bob a loser?"

"I didn't say that," Red said. "He could mix a drink and he stayed sober. That's most of what I know about him."

"Might be something happened at the party."

Red shook his head. "I'd have heard."

"If you give me the name of the people gave the party, I could talk to them."

"No chance."

I lifted the beer and looked at him over the rim of the glass. "Why not?"

"Business. It's bad business. And, anyway, what's your put-in in this?"

"A favor for Barbara," I said.

"I got to take your word for that?"

"Call Barbara." I had a swallow of the beer and choked back a soft burp.

"She still at Mame's?"

"She said she was working today."

He swung a shoulder away and did a freeze. Then he relaxed and turned back to me. "You said your name's Hardman?"

I nodded.

"You the one who was in the paper a couple of months back?"

"That was me."

"You were lucky to get out of that one."

"It wasn't all luck," I said.

I watched the bartender until he reached the phone and began leafing through the phone book. He was taking his time.

Red made his phone call. While he was still on the phone, Hump walked in. He looked like he was wearing about half his money on his back. The double-breasted blazer went for about a hundred and a half, the white linen trousers for about forty or so and the soft black boots for about sixty.

He sat down next to me. Red had his back to us. Maybe he thought, besides killing rogue cops, I had a talent for reading lips.

"That didn't take much time," I said to Hump.

"That girl hadn't sold her quota of cookies for the day. She just zoomed off to the next doorstep."

Red finished his call. When he turned Hump pointed at my beer. Red drew him one and put it on my tab. I dipped my head at Hump and introduced him to Red.

"That Hump Evans?" Red sounded impressed.

"The one and only," I said.

"You look like you could still play," Red said.

"As soon as I get my new knee."

Red knew I was waiting. He leaned in close. "I told her I thought she was making a mistake."

"Could be."

"I told her he'll probably show up in a day or two and he'll be mad she's been looking for him."

"It happens," I said.

"She didn't agree. She said you'd come with good references."

"That's nice to know."

"The party Bob worked was at Philly Chambers's house. You know him?"

I shook my head. "I know of him."

Philly Chambers had been a pitcher with two or three teams. It had been a short career but it had had more than one man's share of the fireworks. He'd pitched a no hitter his first year in the majors, when he'd been just eighteen or so, and there was no telling how good he might have been if the good life hadn't got him.

Seven or eight years later, he was washed up. Too many girls and too much booze. It took Pittsburgh four years to give up on him and sell him to the Mets. New York was like the briar patch to Chambers. More girls and more booze. He lasted three years in the big city and then the Braves picked him up for the waiver price. Atlanta thought he might be worth something in the bullpen. He wasn't. When he pitched it, was an unofficial homerun hitting contest. Only the Braves didn't get to hit against him.

"He still in town?"

"I think he married money," Hump said. "At least I heard that somewhere."

I looked at Red. "You got an address for him?"

"I think so." Red moved down the bar. He stopped where the wash sink was. He reached in and brought out a small metal file box. By the time he was back with us, I had my note pad open. He found the card and read me the address. It was on Lenox Road. The better part of it.

Red closed his file box. "When you talk to him leave my name out of it. Like I said, it's not good business. You got his name from Bob's wife, right?"

"One hundred percent," I said.

I put a five on the bar. He brought back a single and some change. I left it on the bar for him. I finished my beer and waited for Hump to down his.

A wave at Red and we went outside. In the parking lot the sun blast hit me like a hammer.

"Where's your car?"

"The Girl Scout dropped me."

We were halfway to Lenox Road before the inside of the car was cool enough for us to breathe the air.

CHAPTER TWO

The house looked like a split-level gym. The front lawn, parching in the afternoon sun, might have been two acres or three. Or it might have been four. Whoever watered the lawn was waiting until twilight. Even without rain, the lawn hadn't been missing water. It probably drank a half million gallons a summer.

Philly Chambers answered the door himself. Maybe the servants got together and played six-man football on Tuesdays. I didn't have any trouble recognizing him. He'd got a lot of press that first year in Atlanta. And I'd gone out, like about 20,000 others fools, to watch him work a game or two. Until we realized that his pitching arm was a wet, dead noodle.

He'd aged some since then. His hair had gray feathers in it and the sick fat was edging in on him at the belly. I could see that because he was wearing swim trunks and there was a towel wrapped around his neck.

Chambers stared at us for a few seconds and said, "Back again, huh? Well, I guess that means you're really trying." He held the door open and waved us in. He closed the door and we followed him down the hall. At the end of the hall, there were stairs and below us a huge fishbowl of a living room. Down those steps and we were in the living room which seemed to be glassed-in on all sides, the glass covered by miles and miles of drapes. At the back of the living room there was a wide set of stairs that went up to the third level, probably the bedrooms and such.

"I'm at the pool," Chambers said. He headed in that direction. Hump and I tagged after him. The air conditioner was soft as baby breath. It didn't hiss or spit. And it seemed to be set at about forty degrees.

Through a sliding door and we were next to the pool. It wasn't quite Olympic size. About two-thirds of that. On the near side of the pool, our side, there was a single table with a sun umbrella over it, chairs that matched the table, and a single padded lounging chair. Next to the lounge chair there was a copy of *The Wall Street Journal* and a tall glass with about half-a-lime floating in with the ice cubes. The makings were on the table. A bottle of light rum, two-quart bottles of tonic water and a covered ice bowl. I didn't see the limes anywhere.

"I told those other policemen all I knew about it," Chambers said. "That we left early Saturday morning for the lake to do some sailing and that we didn't get back until late Sunday evening. He took away a copy of the list of what was stolen."

I had it then. He thought we were cops. Maybe some of the cop smell was still on me after all these years. I had some trouble understanding how he saw Hump. Hump was the most un-cop I'd ever seen.

Maybe he believed, like a lot of the rich whites did, that you could expect almost everything in the way of cops under a black mayor.

"You put an estimated total on what was taken?" I asked.

"It's hard to say." He lowered himself onto the lounge chair. There was a bottle of lotion on the tile below the chair. He uncapped it and began rubbing the lotion on his legs.

Hump and I took the chairs under the sun umbrella. "What's missing?"

"Cash, some securities and my wife's jewelry ... all that from the wall safe in the bedroom."

"Nothing else?"

"That was more than enough," Chambers said.

It was a smart crack job. There were other things, things we'd passed in the living room, that could have been fenced. But there was a drawback to that. The more you fenced, the more you had to worry. Taking cash, negotiable securities and jewelry, that was the good sense way of staying out of the slammer.

Philly Chambers capped the lotion bottle and leaned back. He wiped the last of the lotion on his hands across his chest. His eyes were closed. "I don't know what your rules are. If you want a drink, mix yourselves one."

I winked at Hump. "You got the breath mints?"

He said he did and turned over a couple of glasses that were on the center of the table. He mixed the drinks. He found the quartered limes in the ice bowl on top of the ice cubes.

"Twenty thousand?" I said.

"More than that," Chambers said without opening his eyes.

"Thirty? Forty?"

He opened his eyes to slits and stared at me. "Ellen's lawyer, my wife's lawyer, is checking with the insurance company now. He'll have a total later today or early tomorrow."

"How much cash?"

"Maybe ten thousand."

I tripled that. Experience had taught me that. If you kept cash in a wall safe with the whole city full of banks you had a good reason. Some dark side reason for not putting it in the bank. That it was money you didn't want the I.R.S. to know about. If you got the safe hit and you admitted that there was cash in it the estimate was usually on the low side of the truth. So, it was thirty or forty thousand in cash. It was a good base to stack the haul from the crack job on.

"You had a party Friday night?"

"That's right." His eyes closed once more.

"How many people?"

"Thirty or forty."

"Any people you didn't know well in the guest list?"

"No," he said, "they were all close friends."

That many close friends? Maybe that was possible. I could count my close friends on both hands and have some fingers left over. Of course, some people were careless the way they used words.

"You hired a bartender for the party."

"Yes, from a bar help agency I've used before."

"Was it the same bartender?"

"I don't think I noticed," he said.

"Any problem with him?"

"Not that I know."

"How long did the party last?" I tipped the glass and had a long swallow of rum and tonic.

"I think the last of them left a bit before three a.m. The bartender stayed a few minutes longer and straightened up and stacked the glasses in the dishwasher. It was something most bartenders don't do. I tipped him for it."

"You stay with him the whole time?"

"Should I have?" He shook his head. "I think Ellen and I took a swim."

"And during this time, he was alone in the house?"

"For ten or fifteen minutes," Chambers said.

It had changed. I'd strayed away from the reason for the visit. I seemed to be doing what Chambers expected of me. I was conducting an investigation. "So, the bartender was in the house alone while you were having a swim. Which rooms?"

"As far as I know, only the ground level. The living room, the study and the kitchen."

It nagged at me. The guess that was forming. "You keep spare keys in the house … to the front door, the back door, to any of the sliding doors?"

"In the pantry on a wall board," he said.

"You check those?"

"No."

"You mind checking them for me?"

He sat up. He found his glass and stood. He leaned past me and dropped in a couple of ice cubes and a trickle of rum. "Why not?"

We carried our drinks into the house. Through the living room to the far side. There was another sliding door and we were in the dining room where there was a table that probably seated twenty of thirty. Then through the dining room and into the kitchen. The kitchen was empty. Chambers led us to the pantry. He opened the pantry door. On the back of the door there was a wall board with several hooks on it. I counted six hooks. Each hook had a key.

"They're all here," Chambers said.

"Spoils that guess," I said. It didn't. After you used a key to get into the house, to do the break, it was an easy matter to return it to the proper hook.

We returned to the living room. I stopped next to a large hammered brass coffee table. It was nice and cool inside. I didn't feel much like going out to the pool. "I didn't see the whole report," I said. "Was one of the doors forced?"

He shook his head. "The other policeman said he thought we'd left one of the sliding door unlocked. Ellen's been giving me hell for two days about that."

"I've been doing what?"

The woman was about halfway down the stairs that led to the upper level, the third level. She was wearing a black one-piece swim suit. The black didn't do much to minimize her size and weight. The dark tan she'd worked all summer on didn't help either. She was fat, fat, fat. Her face was pretty enough. Everything that money could do for it. I couldn't tell what her hair was like. She was wearing a bathing cap.

Philly Chambers looked around at her and then back at us. I saw the look on his face. Hump saw it too. It was that oh, shit look. "Nothing, dear."

I had a final swallow of my drink and placed the glass on the coffee table. Hump placed his glass next to mine. The wife remained where she was. I had the feeling that she hadn't been satisfied with his answer. It would be a long afternoon.

I said my goodbye. We went up the flight of stairs to the front door. He followed us and saw us out. He didn't shake hands. He just nodded goodbye.

In the driveway, looking down the sloping lawn, Hump said, "That is one hard way to making a living."

It was. I said that I'd rather be poor.

I considered dropping by Mame's for a drink. It would be a way to give Barbara my progress report. But if it was busy, I'd have to give it one word at a time as Barbara flew by with a drink tray in her hands. That didn't appeal to me. I'd think of a better way. And while I thought, I circled by Ansley Mall and sent Hump into the wine shop to buy a bottle of light rum, some tonic water and a half decent bottle of red wine. I drove around the corner and made a quick run through Kroger's. Some limes, three steaks and some salad things. The romaine looked more like collards than lettuce so I settled for a head of boston and a head of greenleaf.

While Hump unpacked the bags in the kitchen, I called my girl, Marcy. She said she'd been wanting a steak all day. As soon as I finished that call, I dialed Mame's Bar and Grill. Mame answered the phone. From all the noise in the background the place sounded pretty busy. I told her who I was and asked her to have Barbara give me a call when she got a break.

Barbara didn't call. I grilled the steaks by the back steps. Marcy made a salad with the two kinds of lettuce and a couple of tomatoes and a sprinkle of lemon juice and some olive oil. The wine Hump picked, a 1964 Chateau Moulin a Vent, had balls like King Kong. That's not a bad thing to have.

Hump left right after the dishes were done. Marcy and I sat in the steamy living room and watched the Braves. They were playing one of their better games against the Reds.

When the call came, the Braves were leading by two going into the eighth inning. It was time for them to blow it if they were. I said, "Hell," and went into the bedroom. It wasn't Barbara. It was Art Maloney. He was a friend, one of the few I counted on my fingers. We'd been police together and he'd stayed on after I moved out. He worked homicide and he was damned good at it.

"Barbara Jaynes said you were doing her a favor," Art said.

"She said that?"

"Yeah."

"I was trying to," I admitted.

"You can pack that favor up."

"Huh?"

"The husband's dead."

"Accident?"

"If he shot himself in the back of the head two times, if he got in one of those abandoned wells out in the country and threw about half a truck of dirt on top of himself."

"All that?" It probably didn't make any difference but I'd ask it anyway. "When and where?"

"That's not a hell of a lot of your business now," Art said. "Give the lady back her money. You probably over-charged her anyway."

He could be rough at times. I ignored it. "Where is she now?"

"At home," he said. "Her mother's with her."

"It might be I've got a guess about this."

"You mean you've really been working on the favor?"

"Something like that."

"All right." He seemed to be figuring the time. "How long will you be up?"

"Until midnight. Marcy's here. I don't know what her plans are."

"By midnight," he said.

"One thing before you come by."

"Yeah?"

"Have somebody do a check. What houses have been cracked in the last six or eight months."

"All those?"

"No. The big ones."

"That narrows it some. Thanks."

I returned to the living room. The Braves hadn't given it away yet but they were trying. Devine came in with two on the bases and pitched them out of it. He went on to pitch the bottom of the ninth and the Braves jumped around like they'd won the World Series. It was about as close as they were going to get.

Marcy decided to go home. All it took was the information that Art was dropping by. I wanted her to stay but she must have been thinking how it would look to Art and his wife, Edna. Art would think she was waiting him out so that she could jump into my bed the minute he left. It was all very teenage. I really don't think Art and Edna spent much time thinking about what happened when my front door got locked.

Sometimes I have the feeling that all southern unmarried women grow their virginity back overnight.

That would explain it.

CHAPTER THREE

"It's not much," Art said. His round Irish pancake of a face was flushed and he was sweating. "And when are you going to get some air conditioning?"

"When I stop liking to sweat." That wasn't true. I'd been pricing units for two weeks. I was flirting with a window unit for the bedroom. At least that. The reason I hesitated was that when I slept in air conditioning, in motels and such, I always ended up with a cold or some sore back muscles.

"It's not much, this hunch of yours. A man you're looking for just happens to do some party bartending. A place he worked just happens to get cracked and you've got a plot and a conspiracy worked out."

I was sweating on the file folder he'd brought with him. I closed the file cover and watched a star shell of sweat soak into the center of it. "Since last Christmas, you've dug out eight big ones. Each of these might go fifty thousand or better. Probably better."

"Show me one tie between the one last weekend and the other eight." Art was looking at his watch.

"You read them?"

"Glanced through them," he said.

"One similarity got me. Cash, jewelry and stocks and bonds that might be passed. They didn't touch color TV sets or stereos or the silver. No appliances. Nothing that had to be sold on the street or run through a pawn shop."

He chewed that for a time. I saw his glass was empty and I carried it into the kitchen and made him a light drink, about half a jigger of rum and the rest tonic. I handed him the drink and waited. He took his time. He didn't like being topped but he had sense enough to grab an idea when it flew by. "Maybe," he said. "Or it could be the trend in this kind of job."

"You could check it. Every one of these jobs. Had they used a hired bartender a few days before the hit?" I did some figuring in my head, flipping back through the reports. "Three of the jobs were during Christmas and New Year's. Only two jobs during the winter and the early spring. Lean times. And then the summer and there are three more big jobs."

He wasn't following me.

"Look, Art. Christmas and New Year's. People go out of town or they go to parties given by people who came to their parties the night before. A bartender could walk around a party and hear every plan that's been made for the holiday season. And then three more in the summer when people are heading for the mountains or to the lakes for sailing."

"People do that?" Art was being sly.

"The rich do."

"Three jobs in a whole summer. That's not many."

"The choice ones. They're picky."

Art lifted the folder and tapped it against his leg.

He looked at the last drink I'd made him. A beat and he gulped at it until the ice cubes rattled. "And now I'm drunk on duty."

"Not with that drink. That was an adult soft drink."

He nodded like he didn't believe me. I followed him to the door and switched on the outside light. I waited until he was in his car and had the engine started before I cut the lights and closed the door. I mixed myself another drink and stripped to my shorts. I sat and watched part of a late movie. I kept telling myself that it wasn't hot, not a bit hot.

After the drink, I got into bed. All the bedroom windows were open but there didn't seem to be a breeze anywhere. That was August in Atlanta. All the breezes were on vacation.

About three in the morning I got still. The sweat dried on me and it seemed cool all of a sudden and I could sleep.

Morning. My pillowcase smelled like a jock strap. I took it off and carried the pillow to the back steps and left it in the sun to air out. One cup of coffee and I got some cash out of my shoebox in the closet. I drove to Sears on Ponce de Leon and bought myself one of those easy-to- install window units.

I was almost home before I realized that the air conditioner was about to change my life. Now I'd have to move the TV into the bedroom and I'd probably end up eating my meals in the bedroom, too. That meant the ants and cockroaches might move in there with me. It was, I thought, a strange kind of progress.

It took a few minutes longer to install than the instructions promised that it would. But I finally got it balanced and I pulled down the window and got it locked into the groove. I pulled out the expanding wings. There. That should have been it but I could see gaps. I went into the kitchen and found a roll of masking tape. I was almost done with the makeshift work when I heard someone in the living room.

"Anybody home?"

It wasn't a voice I knew. I didn't want to stop what I was doing. I said, "In here."

My luck and it would have been the IRS man with some questions about my income. It wasn't. This was some dude in a gray hopsack jacket, a green tie and those godawful loud plaid trousers they were wearing this summer with everything. No, it wasn't the IRS man. They wouldn't let a collections man out of the Peachtree office in an outfit like that.

He was a blocky man in his forties. Big shoulders, arms that seemed too long for the rest of his body, and a thatch of shaggy red hair that looked like it had been styled in the last day or two. It was the twenty-five-dollar shaggy dog look.

On the way through the living room he'd taken out a business card. I let him hold it while I finished closing out the humid day air. Then I plugged in the unit. One touch of the switch and the air conditioner was running.

I dropped the masking tape on the bed. On the way past him, I let him hand me the card. I closed the bedroom door. It was going to be an experiment. I wanted to see how long it would take for the room to become freezer cold.

"You're Jim Hardman?"

I said that I was.

The business card was in the name of Southeastern Consultants, Inc. His name was in the lower left corner. George Vickers. It didn't say what his title was. There was an address in the Hilton and a phone number in the lower right-hand corner.

In fact, looking at the card, I didn't have the slightest idea what Southeastern Consultants consulted about. I sat on the edge of the bed and listened to the unit purr. I knew he'd tell me if I waited.

"I had a call from Bill Betts over at Robbery this morning."

I shook my head. The name didn't mean anything to me.

"He's working on the break-in at the Chambers place last weekend."

That was closer. Maybe too close. Might be somebody had the idea I'd been misrepresenting myself as a cop. I remembered the advice of an old con man who said you never told anybody everything you knew. Not even a small part of what you knew.

"Bill said another detective over there, Art Maloney, had an idea about the robbery. That one and the others that have taken place in the last few months."

I got out a damp smoke from my shirt pocket and lit it. I pulled the ash tray toward me. It was his lecture.

"It was interesting enough so that I made a call to Maloney. I got him at home. He said it was your idea."

"I think I saw it as a plot on one of the cop shows on TV."

He waved that one by. It wasn't worth his time. "I did some checking. Odd thing that nobody noticed the pattern. The party, the hired bartender, the break-in within a week of the party."

"It ties together?" I kept it level, the surprise out of my voice.

"In each case."

"A lucky guess," I said. I could be modest.

"It must be more than that."

I stubbed out the smoke. "I think I've been patient. Before I do any talking, I'd like to know who I'm talking to."

"You've got my card."

"This?" I creased the card and dropped it in the trash can. "It's too vague."

"What is?"

"What's Southeastern Consultants?"

"We work for insurance companies. It's mainly arson but we also look into robberies."

"You're a private detective agency?"

"Not exactly." He sounded like I'd hurt his feelings.

"Tell me about it."

"An insurance company we have ties with handled the policy on two of the break-ins. One New Year's night and the Philly Chambers one."

I nodded. He seemed to be waiting for me to do something. A nod was the easy way out.

"After the call from Betts, and the talk with Maloney, I made calls to the other insurance companies that might have had a loss with one of the break-ins. I checked the bartender and party aspect of it."

"And now you've got some more clients?"

"I didn't say that."

"I said it." I pushed up and stood next to the air conditioner. The air had a beginning coolness to it. "And I know you dudes. You charge about eighty dollars an hour. It has to be that much or you couldn't pay for those funny threads or those luxury office suites."

"And you charge a hundred a day."

"On my best days," I said.

"And what's bothering you is that I seem to be here picking your mind for nothing?"

"Not for nothing," I said. "You're making eighty dollars an hour."

"That's a point for you."

"It won't pay the rent."

"You know the total on those eight jobs?"

"The details were sketchy."

"Cash aside," Vickers said, "it might go to half a million. It might be more than that. I won't know until the other insurance companies send over their lists by messenger." He looked at his watch. "I'll know this afternoon. It might go as high as three-quarters."

"You got a finder's fee?"

"It's not that easy. I'm not sure my company or the insurance companies involved would pay a finder's fee, a percentage of what's recovered." His eyes had been locked on mine the whole time, like he'd had high marks in some industry school that told him that people trusted you if you met their eyes. Now his eyes unlocked and slid toward the bathroom. "Maybe somebody else. Not you. You're tainted."

"How?" I wanted to hear it from him.

"Come on," he said, "you know."

"I know this. I've never been convicted of anything. I can still vote and I think I could get a passport if I wanted one."

"It was the cop killing a couple of months back."

"Maybe you didn't follow that close enough. I was cleared of that. If you've got new evidence, do a citizen's arrest."

"Look, Hardman, I didn't come here to insult you."

"You're doing a damned good job of it," I said. I felt the prickling, the mad sweat. I leaned my face closer to the window unit. The cool air didn't help. You'd think I'd get used to it, that it wouldn't matter after all this time. It did. It always did.

"I've got a fund of expense money. It'll be larger after I get agreements with the other insurance companies. It's not accountable money."

"Informer money?"

Vickers nodded. "Out of that I can come up with a hundred a day for you."

"Two hundred," I said. "I've got a partner."

"Evans?"

"You know a lot about me."

"The money's not accountable," he said. "I am." He went to his jacket pocket and brought out another business card to replace the one I'd dropped in the trash. "I think we can work something out." He placed the card on the night table next to my phone.

"It's a nice thought," I said. "The daily money's piss down the pot. We do this and I'd want a percentage of what we recover. It wouldn't have to be a big one. I'd settle for twenty per cent."

"I don't even have to take that one back to the shop. I know what they'd say. Too high."

"Fifteen," I said.

"Ten."

It was what I expected. He was the cut-rate man. I nodded and backed away from the air conditioner. I sat on the side of the bed and dialed Hump's number. He answered on the third or fourth ring.

"Busy?"

"Nothing much."

"The Girl Scout move on?"

"She's dancing in some other part of town."

"We've got work. Come on over."

"Twenty minutes," he said.

I broke the connection. The experiment would have to wait. I switched off the window unit. "Coffee?"

Vickers said that would be fine. I led the way into the kitchen. I put on the water while he edged back a chair and sat. "I can have the agreement about the percentage drawn up later today."

"Your word good?"

"It has been. You can ask around."

"You ever meet my partner, Hump?"

"No."

"He's a mild man most of the time. But he'd hold you to your word."

"I'd hold myself to it," Vickers said.

"That's even better."

I made us a coffee. We sat around and waited for Hump. The sweat prickling had gone away. Until the next time.

"This afternoon you'll have the files on the jobs?"

"Eight of them," Vickers said.

Hump turned away from the refrigerator. He didn't want a coffee and there wasn't much to choose from on those shelves. He closed the door and leaned against it. Vickers was staring up at Hump. From his eyes I could read his mind. He was saying to himself that he'd never seen anybody that big in his whole life. And maybe he was glad that his word was good.

"It might be worth checking Red's file against those jobs." Hump got a glass and filled it with tap water.

I grinned at him. "We just walk in and ask him for them?"

Vickers said, "Betts could ask for them officially."

"That takes too much time. And what if Red says no? The time between asking and getting a court order those file cards might be misplaced."

"It happens," Hump said.

"Of course," Vickers said, "I wouldn't want to be a party to anything illegal."

"You licensed?"

"And I've got a law degree I could lose too."

"One of those high-class types," I said to Hump. I placed our empty coffee cups in the sink. "Let me put it this way. This afternoon, about four, you could be here with the insurance company lists of the who, the where, the when and what's missing. It might be Hump and I could have a card file and we could do a cross-check."

"I wouldn't know, you understand, how that card file came into your hands?"

I nodded.

"At four then." He waved a hand at Hump and I followed him to the front door. He was part way out the door when I reached him and touched him on the shoulder.

"There was some talk about two hundred a day."

It looked like he'd robbed petty cash. Only at his company the petty cash came in hundreds. He counted a thousand in hundreds into my hand. He put away a large wad. I had the feeling that he'd come prepared to pay a higher price if I'd asked it. So much for missed chances.

Back in the kitchen, I split the thousand with Hump. "You know where we can find two drunk mean dudes who'd like to make a few bucks for ten minutes work?"

"How drunk? How mean?"

"Twenty dollars apiece."

"I know those two," Hump said. "Saw them yesterday."

At two exactly, Hump and I walked into the Captain's Bar. I carried a large blue bag from Davison's Department Store with me.

In that big bag there was a smaller one with six danish in it and a loaf of salt-rising bread. Those purchases were from an earlier stop at the bakery section. I'd especially asked that the small bag and the plastic-wrapped loaf of bread be placed in one of their larger bags.

It was another slow day at the bar. Red was behind the bar. There were three dumpy ladies at a table off to one side. They were wearing convention badges of some kind. The bar was empty except for what looked like an evening hooker doing some afternoon drinking.

I passed up the stools we'd used the last time in. I sat on one just opposite the wash sink. Hump sat on my right. I placed the bag on the foot rail below me.

"Drafts?" Red asked.

I said drafts were fine. Red drew two. While he placed them in front of us, he lowered his voice and leaned across the bar. "I heard about Bob. That was a terrible thing."

"Bad for Barbara," I said.

"You still asking questions?"

"Not us," I said. "He's been found. We just came in out of the heat for a couple of cool ones."

"Enjoy." He backed away. He moved down the bar and leaned on an elbow and resumed his conversation with the hooker. Maybe he also ran an escort service.

I drank my beer. Once, lighting a cigarette, I tossed the dead match for the ash tray and missed. The match skidded across the bar and dropped out of sight. I straightened up and leaned across the bar. The match hadn't landed in the wash water. It was probably on the floor. I acted out how satisfied I was about that. What really satisfied me was that the card file was still there. I knew exactly where it was and I'd marked the location in my mind.

Hump and I were on our second beers when the two blacks came in. They were quiet enough. The loud part was the street clothes they wore. Screaming print shirts and tight pastel shades to the trousers. Both of them looked in their twenties. They took their slow look around and picked the table next to the one where the three ladies were. Red saw them and ducked under the bar opening to take their orders. He returned and mixed two whiskey sours.

While he carried the drinks to the table, I leaned over and, pretending to place the bag closer to the bar, I opened it. I was ready.

Red reached the bar. He bent over, ready to duck under it, when one of the blacks, in a loud angry voice, said, "Hey, you, you cracker."

Red turned.

"You call this a whiskey sour?"

"You didn't put any whiskey in it, cracker," the other black said.

The near fat lady, the one with her back to the blacks, turned in her chair and stared at them. It was the shocked, people-don't-act-that-way stare. She even said, "Well..."

"Mind your own business, mama."

Red had had enough. He crossed to the table where the blacks were. "Just leave and there won't be any trouble."

Maybe that would have worked in an ordinary situation. Just maybe. When Red was close enough, he reached out and tried to take the drinks away. His hands didn't reach the drinks. The black on his right caught his right arm and yanked at it. The black on Red's left turned back from shouting at the fat lady. He brought up a bony fist and hit Red on the side of the head.

The hooker at the bar bothered me. It turned out that it wasn't worth the worry. The fist landed on Red's head and she picked up her purse and scooted for the ladies room. It was the hooker's usual retreat in the face of trouble. As soon as the door closed behind her, Hump tapped me on the shoulder. I braced my feet on the stool rail and leaned over the bar. My face was inches away from the wash water. I groped for the metal file and found it. Lunging back, I felt my butt hit the bar stool. I doubled over and shoved the file box in my Davison's bag. Right on top of the danish and the salt-rising bread. A twist and the bag top closed over it.

That was enough of it. Hump had a swallow from his beer glass and stepped off the bar stool. One step and the two blacks saw him. Maybe they'd been watching for him. Hump said, "Hey, you two, get the fuck out of here." If that wasn't enough Hump lifted his hands and balled them into fists. The blacks backed away a few steps and whirled and ran out of the bar.

Hump caught Red under one arm and steadied him. Red was bleeding from a cut lip. Must have been a punch I hadn't seen. Red looked dazed.

Hump led him toward the bar. Red was shaking his head and finally Hump understood and helped him into the men's room.

When they returned five minutes later, the hooker was back at the bar. I'd done my bit by telling the ladies to leave the payment for their tab on the bar. The ladies waddled away. They'd had their wild life for the day. Two businessmen came in and I told them the bartender would be right back.

Red came out dabbling a damp hand towel at a fat lip.

"That was terrible, honey," the hooker said.

Red ignored her and ducked under the bar. The businessmen nodded at him and he mixed their usuals, martinis with lemon twists. My glass was empty. Hump's beer had gone flat. Red filled us fresh glasses and didn't bother with the tabs. "Thanks," he said to Hump. Then he went to the end of the bar and mixed the hooker some fancy drink or other. The in-drink of the month, I guessed.

"Those two ever show up here again," Red said. He was getting over his fear and the anger had him pretty good. He lifted about two feet of sawed-off pool cue and tapped it on the bar.

Hump and I knew those two blacks would never be back in this part of town. They were off in the part of town where they could get good value for those new twenty-dollar bills.

We finished our beers. By then Red had wrapped some ice cubes in the hand towel and pressed it to his lips. He'd returned to his elbow position next to the hooker.

I paid our tab and we left. Red thanked Hump again before we got through the door into the lobby.

The first thing I did when we got into the car was open the bag. I was worried that the card file might have crushed my salt-rising bread.

CHAPTER FOUR

It wasn't a difficult job. Not in the way I expected it to be. The working conditions weren't the best in town. The living room had turned, with the afternoon slant of the sun, into a steam bath. You could touch the walls and feel the dampness. So, we moved into the bedroom where the window unit labored to grab double handfuls of moisture from the air.

We spread the cards on the bed. Hump and I went through them while George Vickers sat in a chair under the air conditioner and gasped for breath. It was an afternoon for beer and we took turns making the runs to the kitchen. Vickers didn't drink as much as we did. I guess beer was lower class or something.

The cards were in two stacks. The first one, a thin stack, was of bartenders who could be called upon to work the private parties. The second group had detailed information about the clients who used the bar help service.

Spread out, both of them didn't take up more than one end of the bed. Maybe it wasn't a lucrative business. That might explain why Red still did the bartending at the Captain's Bar.

In the end, we had six of the jobs tied in. Two didn't fit and it wasn't a match, a full cross-check. It would have been more convincing if they had. But six out of eight wasn't bad. And those six, in each case, had thrown a party and used Red's bar help. The parties had been from a week to one day before the break-ins.

Red kept good, though shaky notes. His handwriting left a bit to be desired. The client cards, below the information section, were lined off neatly.

Date. Time. Bartender.

The bartender part of it was the main trouble. Red used only initials and his handwriting would have made problems for a handwriting expert. We started from the one job we knew about, the Philly Chambers one. The initials there were "B.J." and we knew those stood for Bob Jaynes. The same "B.J." appeared on one of the other jobs, a party before a break-in back in May.

We put those cards aside. That left us with the other four cards. On all four the same scrawled initials. No doubt about it. Hump squinted at the cards. "Looks like an R.T. to me."

Vickers leaned over his shoulder. "Or an R.L."

Both of them turned toward me. I guess I was supposed to arbitrate. I couldn't. It could have been either. So we went back to the bartender cards. I put aside one card that might have been the right one. *Reggie Tilson.* Two more flips through the bartender cards. There wasn't any bartender with the initials R.L.

"My money's on Reggie," Hump said.

"Too easy," Vickers said. He took the cards and flipped them one more time. A moment's hesitation and he nodded.

I pulled the phone toward me. There wasn't an address on the Reggie Tilson card, only a phone number. I dialed that number. It rang two or three times.

A man answered and mumbled something I didn't understand.

"What?"

"Phoenix Bar."

"Let me speak to Reggie Tilson."

"Reggie don't work here anymore," the man said.

"How can I reach him?"

"What?" Then a pause. "This ain't Twenty Questions, buddy." The man hung up on me.

I replaced the receiver. "You know a place called the Phoenix Bar?"

Vickers shook his head. I hadn't been asking him. Hump was my expert on Atlanta bars. He closed his eyes for a few seconds and then said, "New one on me."

I got the phone book and looked in the T's. There wasn't a Reginald Tilson listed or even an R. Tilson. Blanked there. I moved on to the P's. While I skimmed the pages, Hump and Vickers stacked the cards and returned them to the card file box.

Hump closed the box. "What do we do with this?"

I shook my head. I took the file box and placed it under the edge of the bed. That decision could wait a time. I didn't want to show my face in the Captain's Bar if I could help it. If Red missed the cards, he might be smart enough to put it together, the ruckus and the missing box.

I found the Phoenix Bar listing. It was on Ponce de Leon.

Hump double parked outside Mame's Bar and Grill. I went in, out of the bright late afternoon sun and into the dimness. I hadn't expected to find Barbara and I didn't. A new girl, a replacement, worked the two cocktails before the long-drive-home crowd. From the noise level, I figured some of them were on the downhill side of four and headed for six drinks.

I found Mame in the kitchen. It was dark in there except for the lights above the salad counter. Mame was making a sandwich, stuffing slices of ham between rye. She's about fifty and tall and thin as a model. She looks like she could be typecast as the aristocratic aunt in one of those decadent southern movies. I knew better. The real Mame was a Polack from Latrobe.

Mame gestured at the sandwich. "These bastards know I don't serve food after two in the afternoon."

"Don't serve it then."

"And have him pass out at the bar because he drank his lunch?"

I dug in my pocket and selected one of the hundreds. "You expecting Barbara anytime soon?"

"Four or five days," Mame said.

"I was doing something for her. This is the hundred she advanced me."

"She told me about it." Mame knew my business.

A time or two, as a favor for Mame, I'd run down some executive types who'd skipped some big bar tabs.

"See she gets this." I placed the hundred on the salad counter.

"Sure." She carried the sandwich plate to the cold box and dropped some pickle slices on the side. Back at the salad counter, she wiped her hands on a towel and picked up the hundred. "I'll drop it by on the way home tonight. I think she needs it, poor thing." She headed for the door. I reached it first and swung it open. She stopped in front of me. "She said she gave you a hundred. You sure she doesn't owe you part of this?"

"I hardly got started."

"It's a good gesture, Jim."

"What is?"

She stepped through the doorway. I waved at her and went outside. Hump had moved a few car lengths down the street. I got in and we headed for Ponce de Leon.

I remembered the bar front as soon as I saw it. What was now the Phoenix Bar had been a poolhall the last time I'd paid any attention to that particular block on Ponce de Leon. It had been a rough, redneck joint and there'd been a knifing or a shooting every week or so that grew out of the games until the police closed the place down.

Now there was a red bird with folded wings rising out of a heap of ashes painted on the glass front. The bird and the ashes seemed poised on a MILLER ON TAP neon sign.

Hump parked on a side street. He got out and wiped a hand over his forehead. It came away dripping. It was August all right. "I don't know this place, Jim. You want me to wait here?"

"I don't know it either. You'd better come with me."

An old air conditioner had been installed above the main entrance. It dripped warm water on me as we passed under it and into the bar. I couldn't swear to it but I thought I got a whiff of chalk dust. Maybe it was a sense memory of how poolhalls smelled. And then, just as quickly, that scent was gone, replaced by the sweet smell of some bathroom deodorant.

It was a bar started on a shoestring. The bar counter looked battered, scarred, like it had already suffered through a couple of going out of business sales. The bar stools, some with backs and some without, were mismatched. Some tan and some red and some black.

The curved end of the bar near the door was empty. I sat in the space next to the wall. Hump took the stool to my left. The bartender had his back to us. I took that time to look over the bar offerings. Yes, it was a shoestring bar. I counted six bottles of booze on display. A bar gin, a vodka, a C.C., an Early Times, a California brandy and a bottle of Southern Comfort. No, it wasn't downtown Atlanta by about ten miles.

While I counted the bar stock, Hump looked over the customers. It was redneck and poor cracker. Mostly beer drinkers, though a couple were taking shots with their beers. Hump's entrance had ruffled a few neck hairs. Still, it wasn't one of those mean, no-blacks-allowed bars. Not that there were supposed to be any of those left in town. But now and then you got that feeling in certain redneck places.

The bartender worked his way toward us, emptying ash trays as he came. When he stopped in front of us, he didn't blink an eye at Hump. That was a good sign.

"Buds," I said.

I waited until I had a cool swallow and he returned with my change. "Thanks."

"What happened to Reggie?"

He blinked. "I don't know."

"I've been looking for him."

The bartender shook his head and backed away. He spun on a heel and a toe and moved down the bar. I had another swallow of beer and carried a couple of quarters to the juke box in the back. I picked out a couple of Willie Nelsons, a Freddy Fender and a Waylon Jennings. Those were the ones I knew. I left the other plays for somebody who knew the C. and W. Top Twenty better than I did.

On the way back to my seat, I checked my pockets and found one of my fake business cards. If anybody took it at face value, I was an agent with Nationwide Insurance. I placed the card on the bar counter and, when I got the bartender's eye, I waved at him.

He took his time. His whole attitude said that what I wanted didn't mean a thing to him. He reached my end of the bar and put both hands on the bar counter and leaned forward. His eyes were wide in a kind of mockery. I put a finger on the business card and pushed it toward him. He scooped it up and turned his shoulder so that he could get some light on it. After a long stare, he dropped the card on the bar.

"Yeah?"

"I need to get in touch with Reggie Tilson."

"And you're going to tell me that it's important?"

I nodded.

"You call here earlier?"

"That was me."

"Funny. That was real funny." He didn't laugh. "You really want to get in touch with him?"

"That's why I'm here."

"That's what's funny," the bartender said.

"What?"

"That you don't know that Reggie is a girl. Ain't that funny? "

He walked away.

Hump laughed. "You bleeding?"

"From all pores."

We finished our beers. The bartender didn't bother to notice our empty glasses for a couple of minutes. While we waited, I listened to Willie Nelson doing "Blue Eyes Crying in the Rain."

"Two more?"

"Why not?"

He brought the beers. I kept him waiting for the money. "Reggie stands for what?"

"Try Regina," he said.

Hump grinned. "That would have been my guess."

The bartender looked at Hump and back at me. "You skip tracing or something?"

"Something," I said. I put a five on the bar and drew my other change toward me. He looked at the five but didn't touch it. "You know where I can find her?"

"Maybe." He lifted the five and looked at it like he was checking the poker hand. He lifted his eyebrows at me.

I nodded. The change from the five was his.

"That cunt's nothing to me."

"Good," I said.

"Hell, she had all these times when she could work and times when she couldn't. More when she couldn't."

"Good help's hard to find."

"And I had the feeling she was knocking down on me."

"That too?" I said. "Sounds like she left before you fired her."

"I fired her."

"You know where she's working now?"

"Nobody's asked me for references."

I was watching his face. I thought he got the foxy look, like an idea had just come to him. "Not getting asked for a reference...that mean something to you?"

"Maybe. Might be she's going to forget the five months she worked for me."

"How'd she do that?"

"Easy. She'd go back to that bar school and start over, let them get her another job."

"She came here from a bar school?"

"Peach State Bartending School," he said.

I remembered the television ads. They made bartending look like a glamorous life. Good pay, the beautiful people. None of the TV ads had been shot in the Phoenix Bar. Which meant they'd avoided the reality of the job market.

At the other end of the bar, one of the rednecks tapped his glass on the bar. The bartender shrugged and moved away. He didn't look around when we left.

Hump dropped me at my house. I made a call to Vickers at his home number. It was his money and I thought I might as well keep him happy about the way we were spending it.

CHAPTER FIVE

George Vickers called me the next morning, about ten, while I was shaving. I rinsed my face, made a grab for a towel and missed and reached the phone on the fifth or sixth ring. "I wake you, Hardman?"

"I've been up thirty seconds or so." I looked down at the floor. I was dripping water in a neat half circle.

"I made some calls last night. Not phone calls. Visits. The ones I got to, the ones on the cards with the R.T. bartender, do remember that it was a woman the bar help people sent. From what they said, she seemed to know her business. She was pleasant enough. And she handled a couple of passes by guests without making a row about it."

"A description?"

"A tall girl. Looked like she could have been a model. Reddish blonde hair. One of the wives said she thought, at first, that the Tilson girl did her shopping at Lord and Taylor's. You know, that expensive. The wife said she decided later that they were only good copies of designs. You know, how could a bartender afford those clothes and even if she could would she bartend in them?"

"She must be attractive." It sounded like the wife, whoever she was, needed some way to put Reggie Tilson down. Clothing was one way.

"One wife, I think it was Mrs. Prince, made some remark that made me think that her husband might have got interested in the girl. It wasn't anything you could nail to the wall. Just a feeling from something she said, like she was sticking a needle in him."

"Any guess about the Tilson girl's age?"

"It had some range to it. The women seemed to think she was thirty. The men put it on the low side of twenty-five."

"At least we know she's not fifty." My face was about dry. I ran a hand over the side of my face that I hadn't shaved yet. "Look, thanks for the call but I've got to finish shaving."

"What's on today?"

"Hump's going to try out one of his cons."

The Peach State Bar School is located in a store front on West Peachtree, not far from Pershing Point. The two big plate glass windows aren't covered during class hours. People drive by and see the classes, eight to a dozen students, mixing drinks at two facing bars. A sign in the window uses one-inch blue letters. NO ALCOHOL USED ON THE PREMISES. It must be a message for the winos.

I dropped Hump a few doors down from the school. I told him I'd meet him at The Pizza Oven, a joint half a block away. I was at the counter having my second cup of coffee when Hump tapped me on the shoulder and headed for one of the booths.

"Want a coffee?" I followed him.

"I didn't have any breakfast," Hump said. "I might try one of their big ones."

While he ordered, I checked my watch. He'd been in the bar school ten or twelve minutes. The waitress left. I had a sip of the water and said, "Tell me about it."

He'd walked in on what must have been exam time. Between the two facing bars a man in a white lab coat held up a sheet of paper and said, "Number two. Mix a Stinger."

The students went into feverish motion. Hump edged down the bar and stopped in front of a young black girl. "I'll take one myself," he said.

"Not these," she said, "because this is tea and colored water." She had her shaker ready. While he watched, she poured a shot from a brandy bottle and added a stream of what was supposed to be creme de menthe.

"Cancel that order." Hump laughed and stepped away.

The man in the lab coat lifted a hand at Hump. Hump went in that direction. "The boss in?"

"Back there." The man jerked his head in the direction of the closed door in the rear of the room. Hump stepped around him and knocked. A few seconds and the door opened.

The man in the doorway looked like a parody of a southern colonel. His face was puffy and red. His hair silver gray and worn long so that it touched his shirt collar. But the hair wasn't shaggy. Every hair was in place like he'd used a spray.

"I'm Hump Evans."

"John Bascome," the man said. He put out his hand and touched Hump's briefly. The hand felt soft and oily. The hand shifted from Hump's hand to his elbow and Hump found himself turned and guided into the office.

Bascome closed the door. Hump walked to a chair at the right front of the desk. He put a hand on the back of the chair and waited. Bascome passed him and circled the desk, looking him over closely the whole way. "Mr. Evans? Is that right?"

Hump nodded.

"You don't look like a man who needs a course in tending bar."

"I don't."

"Are you from the state licensing board?"

"Not that either," Hump said. "Let me put it this way. I'm in the process of getting together the financing so I can open a nice bar here in town."

"And you're looking into the employment market?"

"Something like that."

Slick and fast. The desk drawer opened and Bascome brought out a form. He placed it on the desk in front of Hump. Hump eased into the chair and read the paper. It was a request for interviews with graduates of the Peach State Bar School. Hump used the pen Bascome furnished him. He wrote down his name and address and phone number. Then he stopped. "This may be too early. You see, we're still looking at locations and the funds aren't together yet."

"I understand." But Bascome didn't seem disappointed. He drew the form toward him and read the part that had been filled in. "With your permission, we'll file this and when you've finalized the details you can call us and we'll take down the rest of the application on the phone."

"That's a deal."

"You're not sure yet how many bartenders you'll need?"

"Not yet," Hump said. "I figure one experienced man, a head man, and I'll see what he thinks we need."

"At least two," Bascome said. He lifted the pen and made a notation in one block on the application form. "And I can assure you that our graduates are well trained, very well trained. I think you saw one of the classes on your way in?"

"It seemed very professional."

Bascome almost blushed. He was that pleased.

"In fact," Hump said, "it was one of your former students who mentioned the school in the first place."

"Really?"

"Reggie Tilson."

"Certainly. She was one of our better students."

"When I met her, she was working at the Phoenix Bar," Hump said.

"I think she could have found a better position if she'd been willing to look around a few days longer."

"I was thinking about hiring her," Hump said. "She'd certainly add class to the place. You know, right out front where the customers see it."

"It's a consideration," Bascome said.

"I wonder, while I'm here, if you can tell me how to reach Miss Tilson."

"At the Phoenix Bar."

"She doesn't work there anymore."

"Is that true?" Bascome pushed back his chair and moved to the file cabinet. "That's odd." He finger-walked his way through a thick stack of files. He nodded and pulled out one. He placed it on the top of the file cabinet and leaned over it. "It must be a recent change. The Phoenix is the last employment record we have for her."

"Maybe there's a phone number where I can reach her."

Bascome flipped backwards through the file. He stopped. "According to this, she didn't have a phone when she entered the school."

"An address?"

Shrewd dark eyes searched him. "Are you sure this is about a job, Mr. Evans?"

"I came here in good faith," Hump said. "I didn't try to get any information over the phone and that's my real name, address and phone number on your form."

"You'll understand that this is confidential information?"

"Of course."

"I'm not sure this is her address now. It goes back to when she first entered our school." Bascome read off an address on Juniper. Hump wrote it down in the back of his checkbook.

At the doorway Hump assured him that he would call as soon as his plans for the bar were finalized. On his way through the classroom the students were mixing Brandy Alexanders. They used real milk.

I had one slice of the Everything Special Pizza Hump ordered. It gave me a head start on indigestion for the day. I could feel the spreading burn as we drove toward Juniper.

I forgot about the indigestion as soon as we met Mrs. Baker.

"That was two years ago," she said.

Mrs. Baker marched us into the hallway. Off to the right, there was a large living room. The parlor where the girls received their gentlemen callers, I guessed. She didn't take us there. She kept us in the hall. Maybe that meant we weren't gentlemen.

Straight ahead stairs led to the second floor. To the left there was a wide doorway that led to the dining room. The table seated about twenty. It was straight and neat and there was even a large vase of flowers in the center of the table. The places were *set* for supper, the glasses and plates turned upside down.

The wooden sign on the lawn was chipped and peeling. There was enough paint left so that we'd read it. It staked out the territory as the Baker Residential Home for Business Girls.

An attic fan whirred somewhere off in the distance.

"Do you know where she went when she moved out?"

Mrs. Baker looked short and dumpy. She wasn't. There was a hint of hardness, of muscle, beneath what seemed to be fat. Her legs, above the laced oxfords, were like seasoned oak posts. There was a twitch of distaste at her mouth before she answered me. "I usually keep up with my girls after they leave. They come back and visit and I send them Christmas cards. And they do leave, you know. This is only a way station, a respectable and inexpensive residence. They stay here only until they can afford a nice apartment or they meet some other nice girl to share an apartment with them."

She'd get to it sooner or later. I had the feeling I was hearing the lecture she gave worried mothers who came to visit their daughters.

Mrs. Baker blinked. She remembered what the question had been. "In the case of Miss Tilson, I am proud to say that I have not heard from her. She was not a very nice girl."

I lifted an eyebrow at her. It was enough to keep her motor running.

"She was an immoral girl. I'm not one to talk. I can just say that I caught her in a lie. And, more than that, she abused my trust. On two or three occasions she left on weekends after telling me she was going to visit her parents. I found out, quite by accident, that she was spending those weekends with a man."

"So she left?"

"I asked her to leave. I have the reputation of the establishment to consider."

"Do you know who the man was?"

"I'm sure it was none of my business," Mrs. Baker said.

"But you knew?"

"I heard that he was a married man."

"That too?" I gave her my best shocked look.

"And you wouldn't know it from talking to her. Or looking at her. Butter wouldn't melt in her mouth."

"When she left … when you asked her to leave …?"

"And another thing. Another deception. She told me she was going to secretarial school. Then I found out that she was attending that school where you learn to mix drinks. Why, I don't even allow alcohol in this house. When I found out about the school, it really made me mad. I can't believe that mixing drinks in some bar is a profession for a nice girl."

"Which she wasn't," I said.

"That's true."

I tried again. "When she moved out …?"

"The man didn't come inside. He waited in that big car of his and didn't move except to put her luggage in the trunk."

"Which man was that?"

"The same man. An older man. He looked very respectable. He was wearing a nice suit with a vest. He wasn't like those other young men she'd been with. You know the kind, the ones who always seem to need a haircut and a bath."

"This man…?"

"His suit looked expensive. His hair was gray but he looked younger than that. I'd guess he was about forty."

"How old was Reggie then?"

"Twenty-one or two."

"I guess she left a forwarding address for her mail."

"Not with me," she said. "Anyway, after she left there wasn't any mail for her."

I figured that there wasn't much more she could tell me. The pump was dry. All she could tell me was what interested her and I didn't find the information about her morals very helpful.

She returned to the door with us. "I hope you find her."

"I think we will." I'd given her some story about trying to find her so that we could collect some bills. I'd swung in that direction as soon as I'd realized she didn't like Reggie Tilson very much. The way she felt, if she knew where the girl was, she'd have told me. It was bad luck she didn't.

"That's an interesting girl," Hump said.

"I didn't think you liked older women."

"I meant the Tilson girl."

"I thought those question marks about her morals might grab you."

We were back on Peachtree. The streets steamed in the sun. Hump looked at me. "You don't seem to be giggling with excitement."

"I can't even smile. Chasing our tails since yesterday and we're not within light years of her. Fired at the Phoenix Bar. No help. The bar school. We get an address that's two years out of date. No help at the Baker home for virgin girls."

"The Phoenix Bar's the warmest we were," he said.

"That warm's still cold."

"We quit for the day?"

"Maybe not." I felt a tickle in the back of my mind. "Might be."

"What does that mean?"

"Find a phone."

He found one and I placed a call to George Vickers at Southeastern Consultants. He wasn't in the office but his secretary gave me a number where he could be readied. I called and it turned out to be that fancy French restaurant in the Omni International.

That was it. That was how the eighty dollars-an-hour boys spent their lunch hours.

CHAPTER SIX

Evan Prince was expecting me. His secretary in the outer office admitted that much. Whatever that meant. I sat in the lobby of Keach, Prince and Boggs for twenty minutes. It was a space only a few feet smaller than a basketball court. It looked like a fashion runway with nice flesh girls passing through in singles and braces. All that made me decide that advertising must have a lot of fringe benefits. The money was there. The whole place smelled of money. Stir in all that sweet girl trim and it must have been a good stew.

I'd left Hump down on the street level in front of Peachtree Center. The wall there was a girl watching station for downtown Atlanta. Hump had leaned against the wall and perched his sunglasses on his nose and nodded. There was a fifty-fifty chance he'd be there when I got back.

I followed the receptionist out of the lobby and down a hall. We passed small rooms on both sides. There were no doors to these rooms. I could see men and women working away. There was no loafing with the open-door policy. And then we were past that and we were in the high-rent section of the shop. Here there were doors and they were closed and there were name plates on them. The receptionist stopped in front of one of these and tapped on the door lightly with her fingernails. Without waiting for an answer, she swung the door open.

At first, I thought I'd walked in on somebody's gay sex life. I saw a man seated behind a desk. He was facing the wall to the left, his head back and his eyes closed. What confused me were the legs and shoes of another man. They stuck out past the side of the desk. I couldn't see his head or his upper body.

I stepped to the side and saw that the legs and shoes belonged to a black shoeshine man. From the doorway behind me, the receptionist said, "This is Mr. Hardman."

Evan Prince turned his head and opened his eyes. "You want a shoeshine?"

I said no thanks but thanks anyway.

The receptionist left. I waited for the shine man to finish. He was on the final buffing, the cloth popping and snapping as he worked. When he was done, he backed away and Evan Prince walked around the side of the desk and looked at his shine. He seemed pleased and he gave the black a dollar bill. The shine man closed the door on his way out.

I had my look at Evan Prince. He was about forty, though it might have been an estimate on the low side. He dressed about thirty. It was part of the business, I guess. He was an inch or so under six feet and he wasn't pudgy in the real sense but I got the feeling that you could do a Pillsbury doughboy act on him and push your finger all the way to his spine. His eyes were a pale green behind steel-rimmed glasses and I got a whiff of lunchtime booze on his breath when he offered me his hand.

"Mr. Vickers called me. I don't understand exactly what this is about unless it has to do with the robbery back in the spring. Of course, the insurance company paid off and I don't understand why…"

I decided I'd better control it. Otherwise he'd talk my ear off. "It is about the robbery."

"Ofcourse I'll help any way that I can but…."

"I'm interested in the girl who ran the bar for the party," I said.

"I see." He lost interest in helping. In fact, I could see that I'd thrown a cloud on his day. "I don't see how I can help you."

"Out front, let me say that anything you tell me won't go out of this room."

"Tell you about what?"

"Oh, come on, Prince. Vickers got the impression that you and Reggie Tilson got past the hello and goodbye and thanks for being such a good bartender."

"He got a wrong impression," Prince said. The huff was in his voice.

"All right." I gave the office a slow look. I stepped around him and looked at a couple of storyboards on the table to the left of his desk. It was artwork, done block-by-block to show the film producer how the agency wanted a TV commercial shot. One storyboard was for a chewing tobacco and the other for a dog food. I wasn't that interested but I wanted him to hang for a time. "If that's the way you want it, then I can't make any promises."

I moved around him and headed for the door. He followed me.

"What does that mean?"

"That if you're lying, I can't promise to keep it to myself."

"That sounds like a threat to me."

"No," I said, "it's just straight talk."

Prince puffed himself up. "I know a threat when I hear one."

"Whatever." I reached for the door knob. "It might be your wife knows something."

"You don't have any right to talk to her."

"From what Vickers said …"

"Fuck Vickers."

I gave the door knob a twist. "You live in Sandy Springs, right?"

It took me by surprise. There wasn't any way I could expect it. He grabbed my shoulder and spun me around. And then he took a swing at me. It was an awkward move and he took so long to set himself that I had time to edge a red hair to my right. He threw the punch at my shadow and his fist hit the door. It wasn't that hard a blow but he fell back and clutched his fist to his chest.

"God damn, I think I broke it."

"Let me see." I led him to his desk and eased him down into his chair. He didn't resist. When he was settled, I tugged at the arm and got the clenched fist on the desk top. He didn't want to open the hand. I worked over it and he moaned some and sweated while I pulled the fingers straight.

As far as I could tell there wasn't anything broken. He'd bruised a knuckle or two and there was always the chance that he'd broken one of the small bones. "An ice bag might help." I backed away and moved around the desk.

The shock was over for him. It had dripped dry and left him staring at me. "You didn't hit me back."

"I don't feel violent today. Some days I'm like that." I reached the door and that reminded him.

"Are you really going to talk to my wife."

"I guess I have to."

"It's not fair."

"A lot of things aren't fair. All I want to do is find Reggie Tilson. I've tried a lot of ways and they're all dead ends. Now I've tried you and you don't want to help. That leaves Mrs. Prince. She might remember something."

"She remembers something all right." His voice had an edge to it, a bitter ring.

I put my back to the door. "You want to tell me about it and save me the ride to Sandy Springs?"

"I might as well."

While I seated myself across the desk from him and got a smoke going, he hit the button on the intercom and told his secretary to go the nearest drug store and get him an ice bag and fill it with ice. He rubbed the back of his hand. His face remembered the pain.

"Tell me what your wife remembers." I said.

"She walked in on the Tilson girl and me. I'd gone into the kitchen with Reggie to look for another bottle of scotch. I was … well, I had a hand under her dress."

I lifted an eyebrow at him.

"It wasn't that bad. Pat wasn't exactly sure what she'd seen. I mean, I heard the door and I jumped away. But she's got her suspicions."

"She make a scene?"

"No. Then she'd have had to mix drinks for the rest of the party. Pat thinks ahead. She keeps her balance in matters like that."

"And the rest of the party … ?"

"I stayed away from the girl."

I pulled an ashtray toward me and flicked off a long ash. "But you saw her again?"

"How'd you know?"

"It's easy. It's what I'd have done. You hardly know the girl and you get your hand under her dress. You don't walk away after that. Only if you're a fool."

"I guess you've got me figured. Later, when Pat was in the bathroom, I made arrangements to meet Reggie the next afternoon for a drink."

"She suggest the place?"

"No, I think I did. I said I'd have to drop by the Captain's Bar and give Red a check. She said she came in some days for a drink. It was that easy."

"And later … ?"

"I'm not going to talk about later," he said.

"Your place or hers?"

"It was a hotel room the agency keeps for clients who might come into town and need a place."

"You gave her a ride home later?"

"No, I didn't. In fact, I woke up about ten or so and she was gone."

"Any money missing?"

Prince shook his head. "Not a nickel."

"Anything at all missing?"

"Nothing that I know of." His lips moved like he was about to add to that but there wasn't any sound.

"Yeah?"

"Well, it wasn't missing but I had trouble finding my key ring. I mean, I thought I'd left them in my trousers but they weren't there when I dressed. They were on the dresser, the keys."

"I don't remember exactly. When was your house broken into?"

"The following weekend. Pat and I were in Richmond visiting her family."

I stubbed out the smoke. "You and the Tilson girl do any pillow talk about your plans?"

"I don't think so."

"Think back on it," I said.

"I suppose we did. I think we talked about when we could get together again. I must have told her that the weekend wasn't a good time."

"And why it wasn't?"

He nodded. Halfway through the nod it must have hit him. I expected him to say something about what a fool he'd been. It was what I'd have said in his place. He caught himself and choked it off. He wasn't in the business of admitting mistakes.

"You see her again?"

"I tried. About two weeks later. You see, I was pretty late getting home that night and Pat had a fit. I had to lay close and cozy until she got over it. I called Red and he gave me a phone number where she was supposed to work."

"The Phoenix Bar?"

"That's it. She was never there and I gave up."

I pushed back my chair. That seemed to be the stage cue for the secretary to enter carrying an ice bag. Ice cubes rattled in it.

I thanked Evan Prince for talking to me and he nodded vaguely. He was in the process of telling the secretary some lie about how he hurt his hand. She was cooing and fussing over him and pressing the ice bag to the back of his hand.

Hump was seated on the wall out front. He said, in his expert opinion, it was a very good summer for Atlanta titty.

Later that afternoon, it started clouding up. It wasn't much cooler and I wasn't sure that it was going to rain. We'd picked up a case of Bud on the way home. We had a couple and I tried to reach Vickers at his office. He wasn't in and the secretary didn't know where he was or when he'd be back.

I got the window unit going and we had a couple more and Vickers called back and said he'd come by. Before he arrived, I heard a rattling, a pelting on the air conditioner. It was the rain. I cut the window unit and I opened the other window. It was coming down in sheets. I listened to the rain on the air conditioner.

"It's like having a tin roof again." I smiled at Hump. "You have a tin roof when you were growing up?"

"We didn't have a roof."

It was a Hump answer. His usual. And I might have followed up on it if we hadn't heard the stomping in the living room. I opened the door for Vickers. He had been surprised by the rain. He was soaked. I went into the bathroom and got him a towel. While he dried himself, I gave him a rundown on the visit to Evan Prince.

"Another zero." Vickers tossed the towel to me.

I threw the towel through the bathroom doorway. "It's becoming a fact of life."

"I'm about to write the whole thing off."

"Not yet," I said. "We could take another lick at Red and see what happens."

"How?"

"Flush him and see if he runs and where he runs."

Hump laughed. "That dude is going to get tired of us playing with him."

"How?" Vickers said.

"You think Red's missed his card file yet?"

"Maybe. Maybe not. It depends upon whether a job has come in the last day or so. He might not have noticed the box was gone otherwise."

I squatted and reached under the bed. I felt around until I found the card file box. I passed it to Vickers. "Find Reggie Tilson's card and the cards for the jobs she worked, the ones she cased."

"Four of them," Vickers said.

I returned from the kitchen with a marking pen. Vickers had the cards in a line on the bed. I sat on the edge of the bed and placed a big check beside the dates for the parties, the ones that were prelims to the break-ins. I put Reggie Tilson's bartender card on top. I carried them to the dresser and got out an envelope.

"You sending the cards?"

I looked at Vickers. "I thought I would."

"Those are evidence," he said.

"How do you want to do it?"

"Xerox," he said.

The cloudburst had ended. Steam rose like fog from the street.

At eight-thirty that evening, Hump and I were in the lobby outside the Captain's Bar. A few minutes later, George Vickers entered with a young girl on his arm. She was one of his secretaries. He passed us without any sign of recognition. I looked at my watch. So far it was on time or near it.

"It still bothers me," I said.

"Oh, shit. That again."

"We should have thought of it." What concerned me was that we didn't know the make, the model or the tag numbers of Red's car. It could be the flaw in the job. But there was only one parking lot. If he had a car, it would be there.

"It's too late now."

That was true. I didn't think there was time for a call to Art Maloney at the Department or time for him to run a check through registration. We'd have to go with it as it was. No matter what misgivings I had.

By my watch it was ten minutes since Vickers had entered the bar. I nodded at Hump. He went in without looking back at me. I think he was irritated by all my bitching. I tried to shake it off. I said to hell with it and went over and took a chair that faced the main entrance. I unfolded the Blue Streak edition of the *Journal* and pretended to read the front page.

Right on the dot the black kid entered. He looked about thirteen. I knew who he was. I'd never seen him before but I knew what was in the envelope he carried. He headed for the reservation desk. When he reached it, I got up and dropped the unread paper on the chair and walked out of the motel. From outside, through the glass door, I saw the kid hand the clerk the envelope. The kid walked away. Past him, I could see the clerk pick up the desk phone and dial a number. That would be the bar number. Red's number.

I crossed the parking lot and got into my Ford. The kid, not seeing me, went through the lot at a 9.4 sprint. That was what he'd been told. Not to hang around. He wasn't to wait for anybody, even if the clerk asked him to.

It was muggy after the rain. Half an hour passed. It was slow, slow time. I got the paper sack from the floorboards and pulled the tab on a can of Bud. I sipped that. Cars pulled into the lot. Others left. Still no sign of Red. I finished the first can of beer and dropped the empty over the back seat.

I'd been waiting fifty minutes when the battered pick-up drove into the lot. It cruised up and down for a minute or two before it stopped behind a 1974 blue Fury. A slim man in dirty white overalls and a Braves ballcap got out carrying a toolbox. He fumbled with the door of the Fury for a few seconds and finally got the door open. He leaned in and released the hood catch. I had a brief look at him. A thin pinched face and dark hair and then the light went out.

After he lifted the hood, I didn't see much of him. The hood was between me and him. I was two rows over and about seventy yards away. And any way it wasn't my car and any of my business. For all I cared, he could have been stealing the battery.

He was done in about ten minutes. He slammed the hood down and hurried back to the pick-up. No battery. So, I guessed he hadn't been stealing one after all. He drove away and it was fairly quiet in the lot.

I opened a second beer. The hour was up. Still no sign of Hump. He was supposed to show if it drew a blank. If Red didn't show any signs of flushing. If he didn't make at least one phone call.

At five after ten, Red came out of the motel main entrance and stopped on the sidewalk. He took his time looking around and then he stepped into the drive and headed straight for me. I lowered my can of beer and ducked my head. I remained that way for a count of sixty. I heard footsteps approach and then head away.

When I looked up, I saw Red getting into the blue 1974 Fury. My head locked. It froze. It took me time to add it up and then Red pulled the door closed. I got out of my Ford and made a run toward him. I didn't get far. I knew I wasn't going to make it and I skidded to a stop and turned away. My eyes swept past the entrance to the motel and I saw Hump there.

The Fury exploded. At first it was a whoosh and then a blast and it knocked me down. I rolled and rolled and there was heat and fire and I could smell cloth burning.

It was my cloth burning. My coat. I stopped rolling and Hump was leaning over me. He'd rolled his coat over his arm and he was patting out the burning places on me. And then he caught me under the arms and dragged me away from the fire.

There were parts of the Fury all around me. Glass and pieces of metal. Fire roared out of the Fury's windows and flared above it.

I'd been lucky. Red hadn't been even close to lucky.

CHAPTER SEVEN

I'd turned the kitchen chair and I straddled it with my arms braced over the back of it. I was drinking my third rum and tonic and my hands were still shaking. I held the glass in both hands and damned the ice cubes for clacking against the side of the glass.

I was bare chested. There wasn't anything wrong with my chest. My back and the back of my legs led the damage report. The kitchen smelled like the inside of a burned-out house. That was from the jacket and the shirt I'd bundled up and thrown in the trash can. I'd have to remember to take that outside to the garbage cart after the meeting ended. And it was a meeting.

Art Maloney had the floor. George Vickers, without the young secretary on his arm, leaned against the kitchen counter and waited his go at me. Hump was behind me, dabbing at the burns on my back with some grease he found in my medicine cabinet.

"You sure you didn't hold the flashlight for the mad bomber while he attached the wire to the ignition coil?" Art had refused a drink. With a drink in his hand he might have been a bit more friendly.

"I'm sure," I said.

"Why not?"

"He didn't ask me to."

I'm not sure Hump really felt it. He chuckled. Maybe he thought he could seduce Art into easing up on me.

"A comic." Art needed to spit. "Now he's a fucking comic."

Hump stood and unfolded a towel he'd brought from the bathroom. He placed that over my shoulders. "It wasn't all his fault, Art."

"You want some of the blame? There's a wash pot full to go around." Maybe he realized he'd left George Vickers out. "You, too. You're supposed to be one of the smart ones. How'd you get talked into this?"

"Nobody talked me into anything," Vickers said. "It was a simple flush. We thought he'd run and we wanted to see where he'd run. It went wrong."

"How'd it go wrong?"

"I think he had me figured," Hump said. "I was at the end of the bar near the phone. That was how we drew it on the board. Red came back from the desk with the envelope. He opened it behind the bar and took one look at the page and headed for the phone. On the way, he got one look at me and backed away. He ducked under the bar and made a blue dart for the phone booth next to the men's room."

"That left it up to me," Vickers said. "It was my job to sit near the entrance so that I could follow if he left. By the time he was in the phone booth, I was too far behind. I got there when he'd just finished dialing the number."

I pushed up and stood. The burned skin didn't want to stretch. "That was the first mistake we made. We wanted that number. If we lost everything else, we'd have that number."

"How long did he talk?" Art asked.

"A couple of minutes. Maybe three. I'd guess he had time to tell them somebody had figured the method." He looked at Hump. "And if he had Hump tagged, he might have said he thought he was being watched."

"He said that and it'd get him killed," I said.

"No way he could know that." Hump wiped his hands on some paper towels and got a beer out of the refrigerator.

"He made a second call," Vickers said. "I got the number over his shoulder. I checked it later. He was calling in a relief bartender. I think that's why he waited so long to leave."

"The way they sliced it, it was close." I carried my drink to the kitchen counter and trickled in some rum and a splash of tonic. I didn't bother with the lime. "If Red walked out fifteen minutes earlier, he'd have walked up the butt of that dude working over his car." I turned to Art. "That kind of bombing. What's fast time?"

"Five minutes. It was the sloppy way. Just planted the charge against the engine wall. From the condition of the car, I'd guess he used about twice as many sticks as he needed. He must have known he didn't have the time to plant the charge below so he overloaded. He had enough in there to blow Red to Decatur."

"It took him ten minutes," I said.

"Slow. Maybe a beginner." A low hit from Art. "But, then, you didn't hold the flashlight for him."

"It made all the difference," I said.

Art had burned down to gray ash. It was George Vickers's turn. "However we judge it ... sloppy ... beginner's work ... any of that, they blew up the road. We don't have anything leading anywhere."

"Reggie Tilson," I said.

Vickers shook that off. "After they stamped Red's ticket the next move would be to get the girl out of town or drop her down a well the way they did that bartender ... what's his name?"

"Bob Jaynes."

"It's sealed off." Vickers dumped the remainder of his drink in the sink.

"Hump and I don't have much to do. We'll sniff after the girl. All right?"

"Until the advance money runs out," he said.

"Two or three days."

"Like the losers always say, it was a good idea."

"Hell," Hump said, "it's closed off that kind of operation."

Vickers shook his head. "For all the good it'll do. Those boys are bright enough to come up with a better one."

Hump followed Vickers out. That left Art and me. Art edged around the table until he found my pack of smokes. "You must be losing more than your usual number of brain cells this year." He shook out a cigarette and lit it. "Somebody plants the sticks right in front of you and you go running over like you're going to put out the fire all by yourself."

"It was not one of my better days."

"You find the Tilson girl..."

"I know. You'll be the first to hear about it."

"It better be that way." He tipped the cigarette at me like a salute and walked out of the kitchen. I heard him at the front door talking to Hump. I stiffened my drink one more time and carried it toward the bedroom. Hump closed the door behind Art and trailed me to the bedroom doorway.

"How's your back?"

"In a day or two we can make a lampshade out of it."

"What time in the morning?"

I said I'd call him.

"Sleep on your stomach."

It was good advice. For the most part it worked. I told myself not to roll over several times before I fell asleep. Once or twice, in deep sleep, I forgot and settled my weight on the burned patches. It trained me. Circus dog acts have nothing on me.

It was a Sunday sort of drive, only it was Friday. An aimless tour of Atlanta while Hump and I talked. Some of George Vickers's advance money was left and I guess we were just going through the motions while we earned it.

There were two big parts of the conversation.

(1) *Was there any way we could find Reggie Tilson?* Not that we could see. We marched around all the angles and there wasn't much on her. The only phone number we had was the one at the Phoenix Bar and she didn't work there anymore. No home phone. And even Red, if he'd been as deeply involved as we thought, only listed the Phoenix Bar number. He might have known another one. That was likely. And there was no address for her except the rooming house for business girls. No forwarding address from there.

"You know why?" Hump said. "She's living with that gray-haired dude."

"Huh?"

"The one helped her move out of the rooming house. That's why she don't have a phone listed. It would be in his name. And that's why she don't have gas or lights in her name either."

"You're so bright, who's the gray-haired man."

"My brains stop there," Hump said.

(2) *Did Red lead us anywhere?* To brick walls and blind alleys. If Red died, as we thought, because all the arrows pointed at him, then the arrows ended at his grave. Wherever that would be.

"His apartment, his house, his family?" Hump asked.

"No family," I said. The hotel clerk said that Red was divorced and his family lived in Texas. He lived in a small apartment in the Virginia-Highland section of town. "Art'll check his apartment later but I'd guess it was raked clean last night…if there was anything there. My estimate is that it probably happened last night while Red was getting his in the parking lot."

"Vickers might be right?"

"How?"

"He said it was over."

❖ ❖ ❖

The hard part was trying to understand why it pissed me so much to give up on it. Barbara's husband, Bob, hadn't meant anything to me and Red hadn't either after I got past the point of accepting the fact that I'd probably got him killed by getting too close to him. And those rich dudes and their wives who'd had their wall safes peeled didn't matter either. They'd get new safes installed and they'd start building the money nest again. So it wasn't that.

Maybe it was having to admit that we wouldn't work it out. That we couldn't find the missing piece to the puzzle.

I did my best to kick sand over it. I spent Friday night at the baseball game with Marcy. The Astros were in town for a weekend series. The Braves won the first game without too much trouble and I guzzled beer and told myself I was glad they hadn't played the Reds. The Reds were too damned good. You had to be a real purist of a baseball fan to appreciate the other team while they were whomping the crap out of the home team. There are people like that. I'm just not one of them.

After the game, we stopped by George's Deli and we had the corned beef and potato salad. The bar was filled with fans just back from the game. It was lively and some of the girls had left their bras home and the bartender, Sam Najjar, stood at the end of the bar during his slack times and winked at Marcy until I had to do my jealous act.

The rest of the weekend was a blur. That was the alcohol. The beer, the scotch, the rum. Taken in unequal parts. The bed had me most of Saturday and the afternoon and the evening was the fog that the hair of that rank dog brought with it.

Damn some favors anyway.

And Sunday afternoon Marcy got mad with me because I didn't want to take her to dinner somewhere. It would have meant I'd have to shave and put on a tie. She slammed the door on her way out. The sound didn't bother me as much as it should have.

I went to bed with the air conditioner on High. I kept telling myself that none of it mattered, that it didn't matter at all but I hadn't convinced myself by the time I passed out.

Monday morning. The coffee in my cup shook like chocolate jello. The doorbell rang. It didn't help. It scraped skin off my ribs. I wobbled to the door and opened it.

Philly Chambers, the retired ballplayer, stood on the steps smiling at me like he was doing a cold medicine TV ad. Just when I'd thought I'd convinced myself that I didn't care it had started up again. I knew that before he said a word. I just knew.

CHAPTER EIGHT

"You don't know me," Philly Chambers began. Then he had his full look at me and realized that I did know him. It confused him and he stepped back and looked at the house number to the side of the door.

"It's the right number," I said. "Come on in."

On the way through the living room, just for a second, I saw it the way he did. The ash trays overflowing with butts and ashes, the beer cans, and the glasses with an inch or so of melted ice and booze in them. All that waste from the weekend. Without looking at him, hearing a hesitation in his step, I knew it was impressive. Not in the best of all possible ways.

The water in the kettle was still hot. I asked if he'd like a coffee. He said he'd take some juice if I had some. I poured him some orange juice and added a couple of ice cubes. That look with the puzzle written on it was back on his face.

"No." I decided to answer him before he asked his question. "I didn't say I was a cop. You assumed that. Think back on it."

He did. I'll say that for him. The soft life and the booze hadn't done in his head yet. "That's true."

I did my waiter bit and cleared off the messy part of the table directly in front of him. Supper dishes from the night before, what I'd cooked for myself when Marcy stormed out. For the life of me, staring at the dried crust on the plate, I couldn't remember what it had been.

"I had a call late last night."

"Who called?"

"I don't know. A man."

I carried my cup to the kitchen counter. The coffee had cooled. I added some more instant and a stream of hot water. I gave it a half-assed stir.

"I didn't understand what the call was about at first. He was describing some pieces of jewelry. It took me a few seconds to realize that he was describing the jewelry taken from the safe at my house. What got it to me was when he started talking about a black opal pendant. It's the one piece that my wife really loves."

"An opal? It got any value?" My mind was full of those milky white opals. They looked about a dime-a-dozen.

"It's Andamooka," he said. "That's where it was mined in Australia. You'd have to see it to believe it. It's been valued at about thirty thousand dollars. It's not just the opal. There are ten or so diamonds set around it."

Philly put an elbow on the table and then thought better of it. His mind was on the phone call. He really didn't intend to insult me. The hand brushed over the table top and came away sticky.

"After the opal pendant, I listened closer. By the time he'd finished, I knew I was talking to somebody who'd been involved in the robbery."

"What's the insured value of the stuff?"

"About a hundred and fifty thousand. That total doesn't take into consideration the increased value of some pieces and the sentimental value of a couple of rings and a brooch she inherited from her grandmother."

"What was the pitch?" I thought I knew.

"He said he'd sell the jewelry back to me for fifty thousand dollars."

"You haggle with him?"

"Huh?"

"You try to talk down the price."

"No. Should I have?"

"It might not have been his final dollar count."

"I didn't know that. Anyway, he said that it wasn't really my money that I'd be spending. He said that as soon as I had the jewelry back, all I had to do was call the insurance company. They'd be happy to pay me the fifty thousand rather than the face value of the insurance coverage."

That might be. I hadn't heard of this particular pitch. I knew that the insurance company was usually willing to buy the goods back. Money paid and almost no questions asked. But approaching the owners, that was new to me. It got me thinking about the other five robberies.

"In fact, he said if I wanted to, I could pay them and get the jewelry back and still collect the whole amount from the insurance company."

"Maybe," I said, "but your wife would never be able to wear that stuff in public without being charged with fraud."

"I thought of that."

"How's the exchange supposed to work?" I felt the twisting in the back of my mind. That question. Why'd he come to see me? It didn't make sense. Not yet.

"He said he'd be in touch later today. I'm not supposed to call the police or the insurance company."

It made the usual sense. If you were going to make a buy, trade cash for the goods, you wouldn't want a bunch of big-footed cops cluttering up the landscape. And if there was a bit of larceny in your heart, you'd want time to think about telling the insurance company. On this deal alone, Philly and his wife could pay the fifty thousand, say nothing, and sit back and wait for the hundred and fifty thousand dollar check that covered the losses. Subtract the fifty thousand payment and you'd be a hundred thousand ahead. But you couldn't wear the junk to the Governor's Ball or insure them again.

The thieves didn't lose either. Fifty thousand was more than they could get by breaking the pieces down for the stones or trying to fence the jewelry whole. And that brought me back to the

other five robberies. It was an idea that might interest George
Vickers.

"It's an interesting story," I said. "I'm just not sure why you're
telling it to me."

"Your name came up during the phone call."

"How?"

"He said he wanted you as the go-between."

"Why me?"

"He said you were seedy enough to do it and keep your
mouth closed."

Even the slime, the gutter people, were popping off about me.
"Did he say why I might be interested in this job?"

"A thousand dollars. I'm supposed to offer you that."

"So, the whole nut is fifty-one thousand?"

He nodded. "Will you do it?"

"Why not you as the go-between? This way they put one
more person into the deal, one more who knows about it."

"At the time I didn't know I'd met you. I thought you might
be involved in it. I said so. He said you weren't. He said the
reason he didn't want me in the exchange was that I might do
something dumb. I wasn't a pro. It was my money and I might
get stupid and try to keep the money and take the jewelry. He
said you wouldn't. The money wasn't yours and it wouldn't
mean anything to you. You had too much sense to buck the
game."

"Thinks a lot of me, doesn't he?"

"You'll do it?"

I wasn't ready to deal with that question yet. "What does
your wife say?"

"She wants the jewelry back. She's getting the money from
the bank right now."

"That could get the FBI involved. You draw out that kind of
money and the bank passes the word to the Feds and they start
thinking shakedown or kidnaping."

He shook his head. "Ellen has an uncle with one of the big banks. He'll get the money for her on the quiet."

"I guess that's possible." I didn't like my position the more I thought about it. If I took on the go-between job and I was still working for Southeastern Consultants the soft crap could hit the ceiling. I'd have to tell Vickers. "What did you and your wife decide about the insurance money? You going to buy the stuff back and still take the full check?"

"No." He looked sheepish about it. Maybe the rich were all supposed to be crooked as hell and he found it embarrassing to admit his honesty ran all the way up to one hundred thousand. "All Ellen wants is the jewelry back." He smiled. "Ofcourse she'd like the securities and the cash back as well, but ..."

"I'm not sure I ought to handle this. Insurance companies usually get somebody to handle the buy back. That's a fact of life to them. Most of the time they don't want to pay that much of a percentage of the insured value. It might be better if George Vickers, the man from Southeastern Consultants, handles it for you."

"That's not the way the caller wanted it."

"Try it," I said. I went into the bedroom and got the business card Vickers had left with me. I passed it to Chambers and he wrote down the name and the phone number.

"What do I do?"

"When they call back, you say that I'm not sure I want to do the buy. You tell them about Vickers. See if they'll call Vickers and do their talking to him."

"And if they won't?"

"If they won't, then I guess I'm in it. You can set it up with them. But don't pull back too soon. Try to talk them into dealing with Vickers. Vickers can try to shave the money down. And the best part is that you can let Vickers use his own money to make the buy."

He saw the sense in that. It was better to spend somebody else's money. Even the rich understood that part. I'd hoped he would. If he remained firm for a time, the caller might back off and deal with Vickers. And I'd be out of it.

"All right," Philly said.

"I'll have to call Vickers and prepare him for the call … if it comes."

"I don't know about that."

"Look, Vickers can't screw it up. If the caller doesn't want him in, then we keep him out. That's all. We don't tell Vickers how the buy is to be handled. And we tell him to stay out of it until the exchange is made. It's that easy."

"You're convincing, Mr. Hardman."

It was a nice thing for him to say. If everything else went bad I could always sell used cars.

I could feel the steam through the phone line. Vickers went to white heat in ten seconds. He did listen me out, only grunting now and then so that I'd know he was still on the line. At the end of it, he said, "I might pay twenty-five."

"That's what our boy on the other end of the line knows."

"I don't think I can stand still for this, Hardman."

"You might have to," I said. "Call it favor for favor. If they don't call you, you stay out of it, pretty please."

"What's the favor I get?"

"I've got this idea. It a deal?"

Silence on the other end of the line. I counted to thirty before he said, "It's a deal."

"Those other jobs. None of the stuff has shown up. That mean anything to you?"

"Some," he said. But he didn't sound thrilled.

"The caller has one dandy suggestion that's part of his selling job. He tells the owner that they can buy back the goods and still stick the insurance company for the whole tab. The other five jobs. How many have the insurance companies paid off on so far?"

"Oh, shit."

"It might be a wrinkle they're working. Steal the stuff and sell it back. Better money that way."

"It might be worth a check. A very quiet check."

"Do that," I said.

"I still don't like the deal."

"I've been straight with you." I reached back and scratched at one of the burned places. It was all I could do not to peel a patch of dry skin away. "No reason to blow smoke on you now. I don't think they're going to deal with you. They know how you people pinch pennies. And maybe they think you might make some guesses about the other stolen goods. That wouldn't be good for business. So, I've got to be prepared. Just in case, I'm going to need descriptions, photographs, anything you've got on the Chambers jewelry."

"I think I've got color photos," he said.

"Send them over by taxi."

He said he would.

As soon as he was off the line, I called Hump.

It was described as a black opal. Black wasn't the right word for it. It had reds and blues and greens in it and beautiful as it was, I was sure that the photo didn't do justice to it. Next to the Andamooka, those milk opals looked like trashy glass.

It was an odd shape, about like a kidney bean. I guess that was because the good pieces were so rare that you didn't cut or grind them down to rounds or ovals. You lost too much in the process.

The other jewelry didn't grab me that much. I made some mental notes but I knew that if and when I made the buy back, I'd base it on the black opal.

Hump prowled the house while I studied the photos. He didn't like the whole idea. He thought there was more to choosing me than the caller had told Philly Chambers. "Those people don't like your fat ass much."

True. True enough. No way to argue with him. I stacked the photos with the Andamooka opal on top. "You want in on this? Half of the thousand for some backup work?"

"What kind of work?" He stopped prowling and stood behind me, looking down at the opal. "You're free with your money. You're the one under the gun."

"Not until they've got the fifty thousand."

The phone rang in the bedroom. Hump followed me and stood at the foot of the bed. It was Philly Chambers.

"They won't deal with Vickers. In fact, the man hung up on me when I suggested it."

"Then it's off?"

"No, he called back a couple of minutes later. He wants to do the deal but Vickers and the insurance company are out. I even lied and said Vickers didn't know about the proposition yet."

A good touch. "So?"

"He'll be in touch with you."

"When?"

"Soon. He gave me an hour to get the cash to you. After that, it could be any time."

"All right."

After he broke the connection, I called George Vickers. I told him that I'd figured it right. They wouldn't deal with him. That being the way it was, my ass was in the fire and I didn't want him mixing in it. I had Hump as a backup man and if we could we'd try to get a lead on them after the exchange. First, I needed to know that he wouldn't blunder in and get me killed.

"I made the deal. I'll keep it."

I said I'd call him as soon as the buy was over.

❖   ❖   ❖

The fifty thousand was in tens and twenties. It was packed in a small leather briefcase that looked like a large bank deposit bag. I had to make a count because Ellen Chambers wanted a receipt. I didn't break the bands. I took their count. I flipped through enough of the stacks to see that, as the caller had demanded, the bills were all used, they weren't in sequence and they weren't marked in any way.

Philly left with his receipt.

Hump and I waited in the bedroom. The call came exactly at five. The caller was a woman. I had a strong urge to ask her if she was Reggie Tilson. I didn't. It might have broken the deal off.

"You know the phone booth at My Cleaners on Monroe near Ponce de Leon?"

I said I did.

"Be there in fifteen minutes. Wait by the phone. You'll receive a call at five-thirty."

The line went dead. I got the .38 Police Positive from the shoebox in the closet. I placed that next to the bag of money. I wasn't sure that I'd need iron. I hoped I wouldn't. But I was carrying too much cash and it would be a pretty wrinkle if somebody robbed me before I got my look at the Andamooka opal.

Hump followed me to my car. "How do you see it?"

"It's going to be cute. Fucking cute. They're going to run me from phone booth to phone booth until they're sure I don't have company with me. It might take hours."

"Where does that leave me?"

"Far behind," I said. "Very far behind. So far back they can't see your shadow."

He stepped away. I backed out of the drive.

CHAPTER NINE

I don't know why they named it My Cleaners. I must have passed it a dozen times and asked myself, isn't that dumb? It might not have been the reaction they expected but it did get attention. The object of it all was a small white pillbox of a building set fairly far back from the property line. It has a drive and a fan of parking space. The phone was on a pole next to the sidewalk. It was a waist high enclosure, not the booth.

I got there a minute early and parked and got out. Hump hadn't followed me from the house. He'd gone his own route. About a minute later, I saw his Buick pull into the empty bank lot at the corner of Monroe and Ponce de Leon.

I leaned into the phone enclosure and thumbed through the phone book. I didn't want someone else to tie up the phone. It was one of the dangers of the cute runaround. And it almost happened. At five-twenty-five, a young girl in jeans and a black tank top walked up and stood on the sidewalk in the shade of an old oak. She seemed to be waiting for me to finish. I put my back to her and dropped in a dime. I rang my own phone number and let it ring until five-twenty-nine. Then I reached out, my hand shielded by my back, and drew down the hook. I held it down and talked away until the phone rang exactly at five-thirty.

The girl said, "Is that you, Hardman?"

I said it was.

"Alone?"

I didn't know if they were watching from some vantage point nearby. "There's a girl waiting to use the phone when I finish. I don't know her."

"You know Gene and Gabe's on Piedmont?"

"Yes."

"Go to the bar, have a couple of drinks. Leave the bar exactly at six-fifteen. Someone will meet you at your car and give you your instructions."

That could be the weakness. I thought, maybe, just maybe, they weren't as smart as they thought they were.

I said, "Is that all?" and then I realized the line was dead.

I got into my Ford and pulled the money bag toward me and laid it across my groin like an apron. I turned onto Monroe. I'd gone about a block when I looked in my rearview mirror. Hump was there, sandwiched between a gray VW and a UPS truck.

That was by the book the way I wrote it. I didn't want him right on my taillights.

Gene and Gabe's was supposed to be a northern Italian restaurant. The food was all right but it seemed over-priced for what it was. The management mostly hired out-of-work tap-dancers and light-footed boys. But the owners invested a lot of time and trouble in putting the place together and it had a good feeling to it.

It used to be a friendly place. Marcy and I used to eat there every week or so. That was before they started getting high ratings and hired a maitre d' whose special talent seems to be rudeness.

I avoided the maitre d' by giving a nod at the bar. I put the money bag on the bar and edged a bar stool back a few inches to accommodate my belly spread. I planted an elbow on the money bag and waited for the bartender.

The only beer they sell is Michelob and they charge the price for it. I ordered one and looked at the inch or so of beer the bartender poured in my glass. I filled it the rest of the way and had a couple of swallows before I got the feeling somebody was staring at me. It's a sweat feeling, the sense you get when you realize you've walked about town all day with your fly unzipped.

I looked over my shoulder and found Marcy sitting at a small table directly behind me. It was a table against the wall and there was a distinguished looking man with her. He was wearing a suit and a vest and a tie. All those things I wasn't. He had all his own teeth and the sparkle could blind you. He was about my age but he kept himself in better shape. He could probably do me good on a handball court or in the swimming pool. I felt a flush of anger and decided that he wouldn't have a chance with me in a dark alley. But it wouldn't come to that. I'm civilized. At least I tell myself that.

Marcy had waited for me to turn. Now she smiled at me and I returned the smile before I turned away and planted both elbows on the bar again. That was it. She'd been threatening it long enough. That she'd find a respectable man with ambition who'd talk to her about books and opera and dance and classical music. I guess she had.

I sipped my beer and checked my watch. Still almost thirty minutes before I could leave the bar. I was trapped by the instructions. I wanted to leave but I couldn't. It might blow the buy back. I leaned over my beer glass. Shit. And then I got a whiff of her perfume, the Charlie I'd given her last Christmas, and I swung around and looked at her. She was carrying a purse. On the way to the ladies room, I guess. In that circumstance, with that excuse, it was Emily Post to stop by the bar and speak to an old friend.

"Hello, lady."

"Are you following me, Jim?"

I shook my head. "If I was following you, you wouldn't know it." I smiled to soften it. "It's just one of those human situations, an accident."

"I wouldn't like to think you were jealous, Jim."

I didn't want to touch that one. "I'm not following you."

"Come and meet Edward. Join us for a drink."

"I can't." I looked past her shoulder and saw Edward regarding me with a sharp, razor intent. Then I saw him relax. He'd decided I wasn't any threat to spoil his evening. "The favor's on again."

"I see."

"Another time," I said.

A few minutes later, she returned from the ladies room. I caught the trail of her perfume as she passed. Not long after that, with an ear cocked their way, I heard the waiter tell them that their table was ready.

I loafed over a third beer. At twelve after six, I waved at the bartender and he brought my tab. I paid it and tucked the money bag under my arm. On the way through the restaurant, passing the maitre d', I turned my face away from the main dining room. It wasn't any of my business. Truth. Hard truth.

I sat in my car for a minute or two. Maybe my mind was too much on Marcy. It took that long for me to realize that no one was going to meet me and give the instructions I'd been promised. Dumb. I stared down the street. It was then I saw the envelope tucked under the windshield wiper on the passenger side of the Ford. I got out and leaned across the hood to get it. At the same time, I looked for Hump. I didn't see him but I recognized the Buick that was parked under the overhang of the laundry two doors down from Gene and Gabe's.

I opened the envelope before I got back in the car. That was my gesture for Hump. Hoping that he'd been watching, I got behind the wheel. There was a note in the envelope. *More instructions later.* It was written in blocky childlike letters using a red crayon. Inside the folded note, there was a single ticket to the baseball game. Game time, according to the ticket, was seven-oh-five. It was the first game of a two-day series with the Giants.

Two games in four days. People would get the idea I was a Braves fan.

It wasn't a big crowd. The traffic heading for the stadium was thin and I parked in one of the close-in lots, the one across the street. Hump's Buick was the third car in the lot behind me. I sat in the car long enough to write the section and the seat number of my ticket on the envelope. I left the envelope on the seat where Hump could see it. I didn't lock the car doors. I got out and packed the money bag under the wing of my arm. I waited until I saw Hump coming toward me, about fifty feet away. I nodded at the car and walked away.

I didn't look back at him. I followed the straggle of fans down the ramp and into the tunnel-underpass that led to the stadium side of the street. I did it slow time. I didn't want to get there too fast. I had to buy time for Hump. He needed to check my ticket location and he needed to buy a ticket that would place him in or near the same section.

Luck was with us. The lines at the open ticket booths weren't long. I passed them and reached the proper gate. I stepped aside to let a few people in ahead of me. I smoked a final cigarette and stomped it out when I saw Hump step around the side of the booth with a ticket in his hand. I handed my ticket to the attendant and walked inside. It was still early, fifteen minutes until game time.

My seat was on the aisle. It was on the first base side, about thirty rows up. It was a good ticket. Those boys weren't pikers with their money.

I was alone on the row for a time. The seats began to fill up just before the seven-oh-five starting time. Twos and threes walked over my knees and my toes and then the row was full except for the seat on my right. I'd expected that. It was how I'd figured it. So, I protected the seat. Once or twice young kids, teenagers, came by and stared at the seat. I stared back at them and they trotted away to find other empty and unattended seats.

The first inning passed. Zip to zip. Morton was pitching for Atlanta. He had good stuff but that could be deceptive. He'd been a good pitcher last year and the year before. This year he seemed to fall apart in the third and fourth inning.

It happened this time by the top of the third. He walked the first man up and the count went to three balls and one strike to the next batter. The catcher went out to talk to him and that was when I realized that a man had stopped just to my left, in the aisle. He waited until I drew my legs up and he stepped past me and sat down in the seat to my right.

His whole head seemed to be obscured by a bandage. It was clean tape and gauze with no sign of use marks. While he settled into the seat, I looked at him. I could see one eye and part of his left cheek. He wore a black windbreaker with the collar up, a white shirt and tan trousers.

He reached into his pocket. He pushed the hand toward me and I saw that it held a box of Crackerjacks. "Have some," he said.

"No thanks." I was shaking my head when I saw that the end of the box toward me had been taped closed. "Why not?" I reached for the box. He pulled it away.

"You got something for me?"

I reached under the seat and lifted the zipper bag.

I placed the bag on my knee and kept my hand on it. "I get a look first."

He put the Crackerjack box in my hand. I peeled the scotch tape away. I opened the end and looked into the box. There it was, right on top. The Andamooka black opal. Under that, when I tilted the box, I could see the flashes of other pieces of jewelry.

The man pulled the zipper bag from under my hand. He unzipped one end, had his brief look, and re-zipped it. He stood and pushed his seat back. "Don't follow me." He leaned closer and I could smell the tape. "There's a gun pointed at you," he said in a whisper. "Don't move for fifteen minutes."

He brushed past me. I turned in my seat. He headed up the aisle. He was limping, dragging his right leg. Crippled. But I couldn't depend on it. It might be part of his act, like the bandage.

I didn't see Hump. I hoped he was up there somewhere.

I returned my attention to the game. Morton had walked the second man. Now he was pitching with men on first and second. He was shaken and upset and he guided the next pitch. The batter got his cut and the ball did the frozen rope trick and rattled off the left center field wall. Two runs scored. The batter loped into third and stood there while the dust settled around him.

It wasn't as if I had much interest in the game anyway. I checked my watch. At the end of ten minutes, I eased out of my seat and headed up the aisle. No one shot me. I hadn't expected that anyone would. I passed through the arch that led to the breezeway where the concession stands were.

Hump was there. He stood next to the entrance to the men's room. His back was to the wall, his hands behind him.

He nodded at me. He looked sullen. I tilted my head at the open door that led to the men's room. "He in there?"

"No." Hump pushed away from the wall. "But you know that."

"Where is he?"

"I don't know." The same sullen, angry stare. "Gone, I guess."

"How'd you lose him?"

"I didn't. Your friend, Vickers, waved me off."

"Vickers?"

"I was set to follow him. Vickers was by the gate. Soon as the man passed, Vickers turned and shook his head at me." The anger played with the sullen and won. "You should have told me Vickers'd be here."

"He wasn't supposed to be."

Hump stared at me. I stared at him. Then, like we'd got a signal from somewhere, we turned and ran for the gate.

CHAPTER TEN

I t was still, motionless as far as we could see. From the elevated ramp that ran around the stadium, steps led down to the parking lot. We were high enough so that we could see across the asphalt stretch to the streets. The couple of thousand cars in this section were all parked close in.

There was no sign of the man with the bandaged head or the blocky shape of George Vickers.

Hump whistled between his teeth. It was a sad, hopeless tune without a name. "I guess I blew it, Jim."

"No. It was a confusion. We've been working for too damned many people. Vickers crossed us and it's supposed to be all right because he's paying us." I patted the pocket where the Crackerjack box was stored away. "And we're also working for Philly Chambers and we made the exchange so I guess that's all right too."

"At least that worked out."

Behind us, in the stadium, there was the lash crack of a bat. The groan that went up from the ten or twelve thousand inside, between a grunt and a curse, might have been one massive, painful orgasm. It didn't change to a cheer so I knew that the Giants had scored at least one more run.

"We could watch the rest of the game," Hump said.

"And waste the good part of the evening?"

We headed down the steps to the parking lot. A hot and muggy night. We reached the mouth to the tunnel-underpass without meeting anybody. Even the smash and run thieves had stayed home on this night. We were almost through the tunnel before I heard it. Even then I wasn't sure. I reached out and touched Hump's arm. He stopped. Our footsteps didn't cover it anymore.

It was a sound somewhere between a cough and a meow. It wasn't coming from the underpass. It was from the ramp that went off at an angle to the left. It was darker there, away from the banks of lights.

The form was against the concrete side of the ramp. It could have been a bundle of rags waiting for the Goodwill truck. Only it wasn't. It was human, knees up, rubber heels rasping and scratching away at the ramp.

It caught on the edge of my tongue. I was about to say that it was one of our better days. All that other crap and now we were about to be responsible for some wino having the D.T.'s. What stopped me was that I stepped on something and heard it pop under my weight. I bent over and picked it up. It was the plastic front panel from a walkie-talkie. I tossed that aside and squatted over the man. I turned him. Even in the poor light I recognized George Vickers. His face was twisted with pain. I touched his cheek and my hand came away bloody.

"No," Vickers whispered, "no more."

"It's me." I put my hands on his knees and tried to straighten him. One of his hands came down and the fingernails scratched at my hands. I understood then. The muscles in his stomach were beat all to hell. It was so bad that it was like cramps. I released his knees and said, "All right, George, you tell me when you can move."

It was five minutes before he could stand. It took us another five minutes to half-drag, half-carry him to my Ford. We worked him into the back seat and propped him against the far door. He didn't stay that way long. As soon as we released him and stepped away, he fell on his side and drew his knees up tight against his stomach. I touched his shoulder. I would have pulled him upright but he said, "It hurts too much, Jim."

Hump left at a trot for his Buick. I slammed the back door and got behind the wheel.

Hump stayed on my taillights all the way to my house.

He'd bled all over my seat covers. I'd worry about that later. Hump carried him into the house like he'd have carried a baby. I pulled the coffee table away from the sofa. Hump put him on his back. I got a pillow from my bed and a warm wet towel from the bathroom.

I cleaned his face. He wasn't cut up that bad. He'd have a fat lip for a few days and there was one tear on his right cheek that might need ten or twelve stitches.

I dropped the bloody towel at my feet and settled into the easy chair. "Tell us about your dumb day, George."

"I thought I could handle it." His voice sounded choked, breathless, as if it came from a distance. His hands were locked over his chest. Now and then, as if he weren't aware of it, he'd press against his ribs. I guess that was to see if the pain had gone away.

"You handled it, all right."

Hump leaned over my shoulder and passed me a rum and tonic he'd mixed in the kitchen. "Don't be hard on the man," he said with that deceptively sly way he has. "He took that beating that was probably reserved for me."

I raised an eyebrow at him. "He did that? Well, that makes all the difference in the world, doesn't it? Any man who'd do that can't be half bad, can he?"

"It almost makes him a brother," Hump said.

"Okay. That's enough. I give up." Vickers lifted a hand toward me. "Maybe it was a dumb move. But I don't think it's over yet. I think we've got one chance."

I had a swallow of the rum and tonic. Hump mixed with a heavy hand. It tasted about half and half. "I didn't tell you because so much was going on. Your toy from The Radio Shack got busted."

He'd caught his breath again. "I know. I heard them stomp it. That was right after they tried to kick my ribs through my backbone."

"You said you didn't think it's done?"

"The walkie-talkie has a brother. A man from my office, Dave Cathay, was on the other end of it."

"In the parking lot?"

Vickers nodded.

"Why didn't he help out?"

"There was no way he could know what was going on. He was probably in his car. I'd called down the description of the man with the bandaged head. He'd make the first follow. I'd lay back."

"So how'd you get boxed?"

"I got too close and I'd assumed he was alone. I was in the tunnel and I could hear him at the top of the ramp, going away. I turned onto the ramp and walked right into the second man. And let me tell you, the one with the bandage didn't limp when he came back down the ramp to help out."

"You get a look at the second man?"

"I couldn't see him past his fists. He was tall and very wide." Vickers looked at Hump. "Not as tall and not as wide as Hump but I think he had metal toes in his shoes."

"This man working with you … ?"

"Dave."

"What'll he do now?"

"We were supposed to keep in touch. If he lost me on the walkie-talkie he was to try my car phone."

I shook my head. "That's two down."

"One more chance. If he's thinking well, he'd call my office number and leave a message on the recorder there."

"Say he's thinking. How … ?"

"Maybe it's not busted," Vickers said.

"Huh?"

"In my jacket pocket."

Hump reached it before I did. It was a blue blazer that I'd peeled from him before I washed his face. It was on the floor at the end of the sofa.

m\Hump hefted the coat, patted the pockets and then dug in and brought out a small black object about half the size of a pocket transistor radio. "What is it?"

"A beeper." Vickers took it and hit a button on the side. It gave off a loud electronic noise. "It's still working." He passed the beeper to me. "Call my office, the number on the business card. When you get the tone, put this to the receiver and hit the button. That'll release the playback switch on the recorder."

"You want me to do it?"

"I'm better off where I am." He settled back with a sigh.

I took the beeper into the bedroom. I went through the drill. The first four messages had to do with other matters. A possible warehouse arson in Tampa, a fire at a Ma and Pa grocery-service station in South Georgia, a call from a girl named Karen who wanted to know when George was going to drop by and a second call from the same girl who was angry that he hadn't returned her call.

Then we got the part I wanted. The man's voice was high pitched. Either he was pretty excited or his voice hadn't changed when he'd moved into his teens.

"It's Dave here. Look, where the hell are you? There's nothing on the walkie-talkie and I don't get an answer on the car phone. I've followed them to an apartment house near Peachtree and 26th. I'm across the street at a 7–11. The two men went in a couple of minutes ago. I've got to get back to the car. So how about getting over here? I keep tagging them and they're going to get a make on my wheels. If they haven't already. The time is now eight-oh-nine."

I replaced the receiver and checked my watch. He'd logged the call twenty minutes earlier.

I carried the beeper into the living room and placed it on the table next to the sofa. "A girl named Karen called twice. The second time she didn't like you much. Two other business calls." I found my drink and had a swallow. I coughed and gave Hump an accusing stare he didn't understand. Then I gave Vickers, as close to word-for-word as I could, the report his man had left on the tape recorder.

Vickers shook his watch. "It's stopped. What time is it?"

I told him. He said, "You're going to have to join up with Dave."

I figured that. Vickers wasn't fit for it and I guess we were still taking his money. "What kind of wheels does Dave have?"

"A red 1975 Thunderbird."

"Jesus." I looked at Hump. "Why didn't he just hand a I'm-tailing-you-sign on his bumper and be done with it?"

"He's young."

I checked my watch again. Time was running away from us. The movement of my arm caused a slight rattle in my pocket. It was one more worry. I didn't know what might happen out in the street and I didn't want to carry the Crackerjack box around with me. Not with the hundred and fifty thousand in prizes in it. And I didn't want to stash it in my usual safe place, the shoebox in my closet. I wasn't sure the shoebox could stand that kind of prosperity.

"Hold this for me." I placed the Crackerjack box next to Vickers' beeper. "Don't let anybody take it away from you."

He grunted when he shifted to his side. He opened the taped end of the box and spilled the handful of jewelry onto the table top. He had taste. He pushed the other pieces aside and selected the Andamooka black opal pendant. He turned it in his hand so that the light hit it. "Jesus, you look at this?"

"Just a rich kid's pet rock," I said. I brought out my notepad and tore off a sheet. I put the note paper on the coffee table.

"What's this?"

"I need a receipt."

"The hell you..."

"That represents fifty thousand in Chambers money. I've got to have something to show for it."

Sweat from the pain and the exertion beaded on his face as he began listing the pieces on the paper. "It seems to me..."

"It's not as if I can't trust you anymore," I said.

It cut. It stung. His face turned red. I didn't want to watch him. I went into the bathroom and rinsed my face and washed my hands. When I returned, Hump had put the rest of the bottle of rum and a glass next to Vickers's elbow. The list was completed. It didn't take much to add up to a hundred and fifty thousand. I checked the list against the display on the table top. It matched. Vickers signed it and I folded it and put it in my wallet.

"Satisfied?" Vickers settled back onto the sofa. The scent of painful sweat was on him.

"For the time."

As we went out the front door, stopping to set the night lock, I looked at him. His eyes were closed but his mouth was moving. Curses. Curses.

Dumb day. He deserved it. I didn't have any leftover pity for him.

CHAPTER ELEVEN

The first pass down Peachtree Road, counting until we reached 26th Street, I was looking for the red 1975 Thunderbird. Hump was driving. His head was turned away from me. He was searching for an apartment house. I didn't see the Thunderbird. Hump had better luck. He located the apartment house. It was one of the huge old ones, about eight or nine stories high. Like some of the others in the area it had been renovated a few years back. All the luxuries inside but it retained the gray stone front. A sign on the lawn, lit by a ground level spotlight, said that it was the Blanchard Apartments.

"See the car?"

"No smell of it," I said.

Then we were past it and Hump started looking for a place to turn around. He was choosey. He pulled into the drive that ran by the side of Clarence Foster's and into the back parking lot. As we circled there we could see the diners in the greenhouse part of the restaurant and it reminded me that we'd skipped dinner in all the run about and hustle.

"You thinking what I'm thinking?" Hump said.

"Can't. Got to get back to the house and see if that Dave fellow called in again."

He knew that as well as I did. "What's in your refrig?"

"Scraps. Dog scraps."

We headed back down Peachtree Road. We were almost level with 26th Street when the red 1975 Thunderbird caught me between blinks. It was parked on the dark back side of a

7–11 store. I said, "There" and touched Hump on the arm. He changed lanes and made a left into the store parking lot. It was a move that almost cost Hump a rear right fender. An LTD with two blacks in it honked him a bad driving award as it went by.

Hump circled the 7–11 store building and pulled in, front bumper to taillight to the Thunderbird. I got out and walked to the Bird. It was empty. I returned to Hump's Buick. I'd just got back in my seat when a man rounded the front side of the building. He stood about six-two and he walked young.

The man reached the driver's side of the Thunderbird. He'd opened the door and slid in and he was closing the door when I rounded the side of his car. As I leaned toward the window it went down with a whirr of a motor and I heard the cock of a pistol.

"Hold it right there, mister." It was the same high-pitched voice I'd heard on the tape recording. Only now, it was even more excited.

"It's Dave, right?" I kept my distance.

"What's that to you?"

"Take it easy," I said. "Vickers sent us. I'm Jim Hardman and that's Hump Evans in the Buick."

"How do you prove that?"

My eyes were used to the dim light. I could see the mouth of the belly gun. It wasn't very steady. It got me sweating. I knew, to be licensed to carry as a PI, he had to spend a certain number of hours on the pistol range. What I didn't know was whether they'd taught him not to get antsy and pull trigger when he didn't have to.

"It's easy enough," I said. "Point that in another direction and check my I.D."

"Where is it?"

"My hip pocket."

"Turn around and back this way."

I did. I backed up until my rump was almost in the window of the Thunderbird. He reached in and strained the threads digging my wallet out. A flashlight flared behind me.

To my left, at the Buick, Hump pushed the car door open and stepped away from it. "What the hell is going on, Jim?"

Dave's voice shook. "Tell him to stay where he is."

"Be cool, Hump."

Hump slammed the car door and leaned against the hood.

"All right." I heard the click of the piece going off cock. "I'm getting out." He didn't give me time to move. The door hit me in the butt and shoved me away. Dave got out and ran the flashlight across my face. The light went off. "I guess you're him."

"It's okay, Hump."

Hump made it a huddle of three. "What's happening?"

"Let him tell us," I said. "Where are they?"

I could hear the whine building. It started in Dave's toes and bubbled until it wheezed off his tongue. "I told George what would happen. I really told him."

"That means you lost them?"

"It wasn't my fault."

"How'd it happen?"

"They were parked on the 26th Street side of the house. They were inside ten minutes. When they came out, they headed into 26th. The light was against me. I couldn't get across Peachtree. By the time I did I couldn't find them. Lots of streets go off in all directions back there."

"When was that?"

"About half an hour ago."

I dug in my shirt pocket and hooked a smoke from the pack. I lit it. In the flare of my lighter I saw that he was sweating hard. "Just now, you were coming back from …?"

"The apartment house."

"Yeah?"

"I talked to the resident manager. He said nobody matching the descriptions lived there."

I blew smoke at him. "And you think what?"

"That they had me made. I was on them all the way across town."

"Why would they stop there?"

"I think they wanted to box me," Dave said. "If I'd walked in after them, I'd have got a broke head."

"If they'd spotted you there are a lot of ways of losing you."

"I think they wanted a sure one," he said.

Maybe. It was a maybe. If nothing else it might have been a way they had of checking to see if the red Thunderbird followed them away. If they suspected the tail. Stopping and starting was one method. Of course, they hadn't planned on the help from the stop light on the corner. That was out-and-out luck.

"They carrying the pouch when they went in?"

"I think so."

"Carrying it when they came out?"

"I think so."

I nodded at Hump. He moved toward his Buick. I said, "Follow us to my place. I think Vickers'll want to talk to you." I took a couple of steps and then came back. "You won't get lost, will you?"

"Look, whatever you think about it, I did get their tag numbers."

"Wonderful," I said. "That's really super wonderful."

Art Maloney returned my call twenty minutes after I put the question to him. I heard him out and made a few notes on the back of an envelope. I opened the bedroom door and leaned against the doorframe.

George Vickers was sitting up now. His boy, Dave Cathay, was on the sofa on his right. Hump had my easy chair. His legs were stretched out, his head back and his eyes closed.

I peeled my cuff from my watch face. It was a few minutes after ten. I waited for a break in the talk. I wedged myself in. "Run it by me one more time, Dave. The make and the model of the car you tailed from the stadium."

In the light, Dave Cathay looked like he'd been to the beach but the tan didn't take. He burns. He doesn't tan. He was about twenty-five and he wanted to dress like those rich dudes downtown. The hopsack jacket, the loud plaid trousers and the white leather loafers. All the trappings. The union cards.

He took his time with my question. He didn't bother to hide the sideway look at George Vickers. The look said things about me being simple and dumb and forgetful. "A black and tan 1970 Eldorado."

"You sure about that? No chance of a mistake?"

He was close to a show of temper or a temper tantrum. "I followed it and I ought to know what I was following."

"That's odd." I did a show of looking at the envelope I'd scribbled on while Art talked. Art had checked the tag numbers with Motor Vehicles. "You interested in what's odd about it?"

"Why not?" Dave seemed very sure of himself.

"The tag numbers you took down belong to a Mr. James Wilson. He's somewhere on the other side of sixty and he drives a 1970 Fury."

"The old tag switch trick," Hump said. He opened his eyes long enough to wink one of them at me.

"That's it. The classic."

"And you can make book," Hump said, "that Mr. Wilson's Fury is missing tags."

I sailed the envelope toward the coffee table in front of the sofa. "And there goes that good chance."

"Have your laugh, Hardman." Vickers put his hands next to his thighs and tried to stand. It was slow and hard to watch the pain on his face. He got an assist from Dave, an arm under his elbow, and rocked on his toes. He was about as straight as a hunchback and one arm was pressed over his chest, "But Dave got his laugh on you. He tailed you all over town and out to the stadium and you didn't know he was there."

"I didn't expect him." It wouldn't do any good to argue that he'd been tailing Hump. "I had your word."

"Now I'll get drummed out of the Boy Scouts."

Dave Cathay laughed. Hump hissed through his teeth. I just stared at them.

"We even with the money?"

"As far as I'm concerned," I said.

"You're making money hand over fist," he said. "Money from me and then a thousand from Chambers."

"When and if I get that thousand." I reached into my wallet and picked out the receipt he'd given me. "It's all right with you I'd like to make that trade again."

"Why?" Vickers was walking now. One step, a pause, another step.

"Talk of money reminded me. Philly hired me. I need to drop that junk on him so that I can get paid."

"I can handle that."

I gave him my best innocent look. "Maybe you can pay me the thousand too?"

"No way," he said.

I held the receipt toward him. "It wasn't your fifty thousand either, was it?"

The logic got him. He passed the Crackerjack box to me. The tape's sticky side was wearing out. I dumped the contents on the table top and did a fast check against the receipt. It was, as far as I could tell, still correct. I handed the receipt to him. He tore it into a dozen scraps and let it flutter in the general direction of the ashtray.

"What now, George?"

"The crime rate at the stadium just went up ten points. It seems I got mugged there tonight."

"Where'll you be?"

"At Grady Hospital for the next hour or two ... if they don't keep me overnight."

"Call me in the morning."

He said he would. He braced shoulders with Dave Cathay and they went down the front steps. I let them reach the walk before I cut the light and closed the door.

"I like that Dave," Hump said. "I'd like to finish raising him if I had the time."

"It's a thankless job," I said. I was tired of the Crackerjack box. I carried the handful of jewelry to the kitchen and tore a paper towel from the roll. I wrapped the pieces in the towel and put it in my jacket pocket.

Hump followed me into the kitchen. "You going over there tonight?"

"I think Philly might be interested in how it turned out."

"Funny he hasn't called."

"He's probably saying the same thing about me."

Hump stretched and yawned. "You want me along?"

"Not unless you want to. You fixed with cash?"

"I can last until tomorrow."

The phone rang in the bedroom. Hump had started for the front door. I caught the phone on the fourth ring. I looked around and saw Hump in the doorway.

"Jim?" It was Marcy.

Hump lifted an eyebrow at me. Was it important? I shook my head and he waved and I heard the front door close behind him.

"Yes?"

"I wanted to be sure you were okay."

"I'm fine," I said.

"You sound far away. Like you're a mile from the phone."

"Sorry." I stretched my arm and the cuff moved back. I read the time. "That was a short date."

"It wasn't really a date. Edward's a new friend at the office. We have a lot to talk about."

"I'll bet," I said.

"He's just a friend."

"You tell him that?"

"I'm telling you," Marcy said.

"In a day or two remember that I didn't ask."

"Poor baby."

That was supposed to jolly me. "That's right."

"Poor baby, you got your feelings hurt."

"Some."

"I can come over." It was tentative. It had the right amount of hesitation in it.

"I'm on my way out."

"I see." Now she was the poor baby.

"No, I'm finishing up that favor."

"Can't you do that tomorrow?"

"It's payday."

"All right, Jim."

There was a hurt resignation in her voice. I should have expected to hear the click when she broke the connection. I didn't. It surprised me and I stood there and listened to the dead line for a few seconds.

I was fixed by the harsh light of the front porch. I blinked into it. I knew that that kind of lighting didn't make me look any friendlier or any less dangerous.

"Do I know you?" Ellen Chambers said. I couldn't see her but I could see the eye at the spyhole in the door.

I gave her my name. "I was here a week ago and talked to your husband."

"You're police?"

"No." I fought back the irritation. "Look, either let me in or call Philly. I've got the jewelry for him. I did the buy back this evening."

"Oh, you're *that* man?"

I said I was. I reached into my jacket pocket and brought out the wad of paper towel. "Can you see these?" I held the jumble of pieces toward the spyhole.

"Not too well."

I stuck a finger in the pile and selected the black opal. "This?"

"Yes." There was a wait and then I heard the first lock. A snick and then another one. They'd made the split level a fortress. Either it had been that way the whole time or they'd had the locksmith in after the robbery. "I suppose it's all right."

The door opened wide enough for me to slide through sideways. When I was in the hall I stepped to the side to let her close the door. As she moved away, I smelled soap. No perfume or cologne. Just soap. Ellen Chambers was wearing a dark red house robe that would have been a tent for a small circus. Her hair, which had been under a bathing cap my other visit, was in some kind of sleep net. I could see enough of it to know that it had been doctored to platinum blond. That cheap look. Maybe that was the way Philly liked it. If he liked her hair at all or anything about her. I had a flash of that look on his face the time she'd come down the stairs and surprised him.

"Where's Philly?"

"He's not here right now."

I could see that. Some people have a love of the obvious.

She'd been looking at me. I guess she decided that I didn't have rape on my mind. She dipped her head toward the stairs that led to the living room level. I let her lead the way. I watched the way she moved. For a big woman there was a certain amount of grace. There was a good chance she'd learned to move that way in a finishing school. I could hear the teachers over their coffee break. *If Ellen's going to stay fat, it might as well be majestic fat.*

I stopped at the bottom of the stairs. She continued on and reached the sofa. "When do you expect him? I've got business with him."

"You have the jewelry?"

I moved closer to her and held out the wad of paper towel.

"I can handle any business he has with you."

She put her back to me and carried the jewelry to the sofa. She sat and then remembered me. She leaned forward and pulled the hem of her house robe together and lapped it over her knees. I kept my distance. I waited while she unloaded the paper towel, piece by piece. It took her several minutes. For her, it wasn't like counting apples and oranges. Now and then she'd stop to admire one of the pieces and hold it to the light.

Finally, she nodded. "They're all here."

"It's good to know."

She stood. "I want to thank you, Mr. Hardman." It was the dismissal. The goodbye.

"Maybe I'd better wait for Philly, Mrs. Chambers."

"I can't say when he'll be back."

"I've got some business to complete with him."

"I've said I could handle any business you have with him."

It was getting on my nerves. This going about in circles. "My business with him concerns a thousand dollars."

"He paid you."

"No."

"He had a receipt. I'd insisted upon a receipt."

"The receipt was for the fifty thousand. I was supposed to get a thousand for being the go-between."

"I don't like to suggest that you're lying."

"I'd rather you didn't suggest that," I said. "Tell me where he is and I'll have my talk with him."

"He won't be back until tomorrow."

"Where is he?"

"He's in New York," she said.

"Then I guess I can't do my business with him tonight. Nothing I can do about that. But I gave you a receipt for the fifty thousand. If I can't be paid tonight what I want is a receipt for the stuff I brought back. That you received it all."

"I can do that."

I passed my note pad to her. She fumbled for a pen. I passed my pen to her as well. I stood over her while she scribbled a short statement that all the pieces of jewelry had been received from James Hardman "in excellent condition." She signed it with a flourish. She passed the pad to me. I read it through before I nodded. It was a girlish handwriting, the round loops and the circular dots over the "I's".

I said that I'd taken enough of her time. I headed for the stairs. At the top, in the hallway, I said, "The trip to New York, he didn't say anything to me about it when he dropped off the money."

"It was unexpected." She mounted the stairs and stepped past me. "He said the call came a few minutes before six."

"Business?"

"It was the Mets. There's a chance for him in the organization, something in the front office."

I reached the door. "They work like that? It's midseason."

"I think someone resigned."

"I guess that happens." I opened the door. The hot damp air rolled past me.

Behind me, as I went down the steps, she filled a good part of the doorway. "I hope, Mr. Hardman, that you won't think that I'm unappreciative."

"Not at all."

"Perhaps I misunderstood Philly."

"It'll work out," I said.

On the drive back to town I wasn't that calm. That bastard, Philly. Unless it was a misunderstanding. If it wasn't, if that washed-up jock was playing games, I'd put Hump on him until he decided that a thousand dollars wasn't a lot of money at all.

Anger gave me a stomach burn. I didn't like being taken for a fish.

CHAPTER TWELVE

I spent the long late morning hours on my back steps. Part of the time I considered doing something with the yard. The rest of the time I spent talking myself out of it. And between cups of coffee I walked around the house and inspected the fig tree. The rain a few days before had helped some. The figs appeared to be increasing in size. It would be a week or so before I knew if the fruit would mature. If it didn't there would be none of the fig preserves Marcy liked to make. The ones I liked with breakfast. Marcy has a way of cooking the figs with sugar and honey and ginger and lemon peel. It's an old Southern recipe.

The figs brought me back to Marcy. It wasn't any of my business, of course, that she had drinks and dinner with some man. No ring, no paper said she couldn't. Even when it pissed me that the man had looked at me like he thought I was her uncle.

It was a logical progression from Marcy to the money Philly Chambers owed me. Not that the shoe-box was low. It wasn't. But that thousand was *found* money, payment for a rotten, frustrating evening. If I had my half of that thousand and if Marcy would talk to me, it might be a good weekend for a drive into the mountains. Maybe even as far as North Carolina if we wanted to. All the way to Blowing Rock.

I know a man owns a house there in the Mayfair Manor part of town. It's built of native stone and it has a wide porch that overlooks the valley and it has a tin roof. My name's still on a list he leaves with the caretaker. If it's not being used, I'm free to pick up the key.

On cool mornings the fog flows up from the valley below and it covers the mountains. And usually it rains in the early morning and the sound of the rain on that tin roof makes me feel like a child again, like I'm an innocent with all the crap scraped away.

You need a blanket those mornings. It's warm in that big bed and most of the warmth is from the woman next to you.

I ropewalked around the thousand dollars until noon. I had a sandwich and then I made a fresh cup of coffee and carried it into the bedroom. I sat on the bed and leaned over and ran a hand under the bed. I was looking for the phone book. I didn't find it but I found Red's card file box. It was slick with floor dust and a light touch and it slid out and lodged against my shoe. I flipped up the lid and there they were, the five cards we'd put aside and xeroxed. The flush message for Red. The five cards were held together by a rubber band.

The top card was Reggie Tilson's. I slipped the band and found Philly Chamber's card. I realized I didn't need the phone book. Philly's number was under the street address. I dropped the other cards back in the file box. I dialed the Chambers number from the card.

A young woman answered. It wasn't Ellen. "Miz Chambers' residence."

I gave my name. It was a minute or so of wait.

"Yes?"

Odd. Close to her, in person, I didn't hear it. She really didn't have a Southern accent. It was soft in some of the right places and the modulations weren't far off. But it wasn't Southern. It had the iron steel ridge of the North in there.

"I wondered if you've heard when Philly's coming back."

"Is this Mr. Hardman?"

"I gave the girl my name," I said.

There was a hesitation. I almost felt the breath, the small stir that her lip movement made. "I think I need to talk to you, Mr. Hardman."

Now I backed away. "I don't see any point to it. I don't want to get in this nonsense about how you can handle any of the business that Philly can. I don't feel like chasing that around the room again. I'll do my talking with Philly."

"I understand. It's not that. It's about Philly."

"What about him?"

"I don't want to talk about it over the phone. Could you be here in an hour and a half?"

"I can be there in half an hour," I said.

"I want my lawyer here when we talk. I'll have to call and make certain he can be here."

"If it's about the thousand dollars..." I had a hunch the talk about the lawyer might be her way of trying to run me away. It was the wealthy's method of dealing with someone they thought was bothering them.

"It's not. In fact, in the circumstances, I believe I can give you a check to cover what Philly owed you."

Much better.

She asked for my number and I read it off the phone dial. She said she'd call back as soon as she reached her lawyer. I said I'd wait for her call.

I had a slow careful shave and a dip under the shower. I dressed with care. I picked out a tie that didn't have sweat wrinkles, a white shirt and the tan suit that was still in the cleaner bag.

The phone rang while I was putting on my socks. That was fast.

It wasn't Ellen Chambers. It was George Vickers.

"How you feeling, George?"

"Okay, if you don't count that row of catgut whiskers that grows on one side of my face."

"How many stitches?"

"I quit counting at fifteen."

"Look on the good side of it," I said. "Now you can tell those girls you got the scar in a backstreet duel with some dangerous criminal."

"Not likely. The company'll pay for plastic surgery." I heard the hiss-flare of a match while he lit a smoke. "Look, I think you sent me down a wrong road."

"What road was that?"

"The new wrinkle you thought those break-in boys had."

"They had two or …"

"Selling the stuff back to the people they robbed it from."

"That one," I said.

"I checked it out. I decided not to pussyfoot about it. I saw two of the families this morning and I sent Dave … you remember Dave, don't you?"

I said, "How could I ever forget him?"

"Well, a lot of talk and I'm pretty sure none of them were approached with the buy back or the chance to defraud the insurance companies."

"It's like that, George. Sometimes you don't get a good hunch even once a month."

"I thought you'd want to know. That was the favor you traded me."

"Don't sound so cheated."

"Huh?"

"Your part of the favor, what I traded you the bad hunch for, was that you'd stay out of the buy back last night."

"You're right about that." A pause. "You keep score, Hardman."

"It's one of the simple pleasures."

"Are we even now?"

I said I thought we were.

"Keep in touch."

I said I would. Both of us knew that we wouldn't. I wouldn't and he wouldn't. With good reason. I decided, just before I broke the connection, that we really didn't like each other very much.

It was two o'clock. I sat on the sofa in the living room at the Chambers house. Ellen Chambers was on my right. Across the table from us sat her lawyer, an old and distinguished man named Frank Butler. I'd never met Butler before but I knew who he was. His name showed up in the papers from time to time. He was part of the invisible power structure of the city. At least, he'd had that power when they'd controlled the Mayor's office and the City Council. Now, with a black Mayor and a black-white split in the City Council, he'd lost some of his dignity. He spent most of his time yapping at the Mayor's heels, bitching about downtown crime and the economic fears of the down-town merchants.

Still, it impressed me that Ellen Chambers had him as a law-yer. It moved her stock portfolio, in my mind, up a million or so and it meant that she'd either come from a family with money or a family with very good social ties.

I'd asked for a Scotch rocks. It came in fine crystal and it was the real dew. The single malt. Butler didn't take a drink when it was offered. And when she'd mixed my drink, from the looks of her glass, she'd made herself a Shirley Temple just to keep me company.

"I suppose I should begin it," Ellen Chambers said.

Frank Butler had been reading me like a stock offering. I guess I barely passed. I wasn't as seedy as usual. The lapels on my suit jacket were a bit wide for this year but they'd been fine last year. And I'd given my shoes a brush. If any of that shit mattered.

"With the usual proviso," Frank Butler said.

I'd been around enough to understand him. That fancy language. "You've got it," I said. I looked at Ellen Chambers and saw that she had a puzzled stare on her face. "What I mean is that I'm not going to broadcast anything that's said to me here."

"In all fairness," Frank Butler said, "I have to say that I don't exactly approve of this. If Ellen wants to hire someone, I would be glad to ..."

I lost track of him. I swung my head to my right. Yes, her face said, he's speaking for me. He hasn't misunderstood.

"... however believes that the way in which you handled the recovery of her jewelry means that she can trust you." He lifted a thin leather briefcase from the coffee table. "And that reminds me. I've taken the liberty of having this check drawn up." The smooth glide of the zipper. "If you prefer, I could have this check certified ..."

I said that I thought his check was probably good. I took the check and glanced at it and placed it on the table in front of me. The check had been written on a check writer and it was for a thousand dollars.

"I will be dealing with the insurance company about the replacement of the money that was paid to recover the jewelry and I think I can argue that your fee was a legitimate part of the expense."

I was fairly sure that he'd make it stick. I was tempted to give him another card to play. That Vickers had hired me, that Vickers had the tie-in with the insurance companies. I stopped myself. I didn't like Vickers and I didn't like the way he'd played with me but I wasn't sure I wanted to put in a bind.

"And that brings us to the other business."

Butler dipped his head toward Ellen Chambers. It was her turn at the podium.

"I wasn't lying to you last night, Mr. Hardman. When I talked to you, I really did believe that Philly was in New York. This morning, partly because of my talk with you, I called the

Berkshire Hotel. He'd said he'd be staying there. It turns out that he isn't registered there and they don't have a reservation for him."

The pause wasn't for me to say something. I could see her throat muscles working. It was hard on her and she needed a few seconds to compose herself. And I thought I detected a misting in her eyes.

"So … so … I called the Mets front office. I know a Mr. Jacobs there. He's an old family friend. He was surprised by my call. He said he hadn't been in touch with Philly and that they hadn't been considering him for a position."

Butler stirred in his chair. He coughed. He'd seen what I had and he stepped in to rescue her by doing some of the rest of the explanation.

"Ellen called me. That was earlier this morning. I used my resources to do some checking for her. He'd told her that he was taking a seven-twenty flight from Hartsfield. A check was made on all flights that left Atlanta between seven and eight in the evening. Philip wasn't on the lists for any of the flights. I even took the liberty of going beyond the eight o'clock deadline. He didn't leave Atlanta by plane last night."

"So, you think he's still in town?" I didn't know what the question really meant but I felt I ought to show that I wasn't deaf and dumb.

"Ellen believes he is."

"Maybe he left by car."

"His car is in the garage," Ellen said. "He took a cab to the airport. I offered to drive him but he said he'd rather take the cab."

"You notice which cab company it was?"

"I called it for him. He was packing a few things for the trip. It was the Terminal City cab company."

"What time?"

"It was six-thirty when the cab arrived."

I could try a check on that. Some cab companies kept better trip records than others did. It was a thin, thin chance. "How was he fixed for money?"

That was the standard question. It was important. It was also the one that deserted husbands and wives didn't like to answer. Whatever the reason was. I'd never understood.

"He has his own checking account," she said. "I called the bank this morning and spoke to my uncle. He said there is a balance of about six hundred in that account but that might not show any checks written in the last few days."

"Cash on hand? Credit cards?"

"He has the usual credit cards. I'm not sure how much cash he had with him. He usually carried a hundred or so in spending money." She blinked at me. "And he had the thousand dollars that he was supposed to have paid you in advance."

"And there is one more matter," Frank Butler said.

Ellen wanted to stop me. "Do you think … ?"

"If you insist on hiring Mr. Hardman, the least you can do is give him all the information you have." He faced me. "Am I right in thinking that the amount of money the … missing man has would dictate to some degree where you would look for him?"

It wasn't exactly how I'd phrase it. I nodded.

"This part is certainly confidential," Butler said.

I nodded again.

"I was trying to decide how to approach Ellen with this matter. I was about to call her this morning when she called me. The circumstances, Philip leaving, made it much easier for me. In brief, I've been considering a call to the insurance company since lunchtime yesterday. That call would ask the insurance company to reduce the value of the materials stolen from the safe upstairs."

"That went past me," I said.

"I had lunch with a friend yesterday. He is an officer with a bank I'd rather not name. In conversation it came up that Philip had borrowed a sizable amount on a block of stock owned jointly by Philip and Ellen. My friend asked if the Chamberses were having financial difficulties. I assured him that they weren't."

"How much?"

"It was a considerable amount."

"Fifty thousand?" I said.

He didn't blink.

"A hundred thousand."

He didn't deny that I was getting warm. He ignored it altogether. "It would seem that Philip, sometime prior to the time when the safe was robbed, took those securities for his own purposes."

"And he forged Mrs. Chamber's signature for the bank transaction?"

He nodded.

It ran up on me and hit me a good lick right in the tricky part of my mind. Dogshit. Merry dogshit. Oh, this is a good one. And then I put my head back and hooted. A wild hoot. One that could have been heard across the valley at Blowing Rock.

Both of them looked at me like I'd gone crazy. I choked the hoot and took a couple of deep breaths. "I've got a couple of questions for you, Mrs. Chambers."

The amazed look hadn't left her face. "If I can."

"I need the real answer to this one. How much cash was really kept in the upstairs safe?"

"Is it really important?"

"You'll understand in a minute," I said.

"It was somewhere between twenty and twenty-five thousand dollars. I can't be sure."

"What's behind this kind of question?" Frank Butler said. There was an angry edge to his voice. Maybe he thought I was playing games with Ellen Chambers.

I let them wait. I'd seen a couple of stage plays in my time. Those times when Marcy got the tickets and insisted I go with her. There always seemed to be a strong line at the end of an act. A zinger of a line. I picked up my drink and tipped it back until the ice rattled against my teeth.

"Tell me about the time you had a party... it would have been two or three months ago... and you got a bartender from the bar help service and it turned out to be a woman. A blonde, a very attractive young woman."

CHAPTER THIRTEEN

I walked across the lawn to my old Ford. It was what you'd call a beautiful August day, if you liked August in Atlanta. After the drought, the new green mist was on everything. It showed what a rain or two would do.

The sun was at an angle, quartering away. And then, after the freezer box level of the air conditioning inside, the first sweat broke with the sting of a sand storm. Maybe it wasn't just the sun. It could have been partly shame.

The question I'd asked. It had been a punch in the mouth. I'd seen the stunned look on Ellen Chambers's face. It was the stir-together of the surprise and the fatalistic knowledge that a lamb must get when he reaches the bottom of the chute at the slaughterhouse and realizes it isn't the goat that's ringing the bell.

Yes, I remember the girl.

"Anything happen that night?"

Nothing that I noticed.

"But now you think…"

I am a realistic person, Mr. Hardman. I was brought up to be. Philip could be a very charming person if he wanted to be. When he wanted to be. During the six years we've been married, I believe I've known each time he's been with another woman. I've comforted myself with the thought that these women didn't really matter to him. They lasted one night or perhaps even two. A long weekend at the most.

"When was the party?"

It was May 14th.

My mouth must have dropped open.

I guess you're surprised that I remember the exact date.

"Yes."

It is a hard date to forget. The party was to celebrate the sixth anniversary of our wedding.

"A good party?" Dumb question but I couldn't come up with anything else.

It seemed to be at the time. In fact, without realizing it, I've drawn a line under that date. Since May, since that time, Philip has been different. Quieter, more introspective. I didn't understand it, but I accepted it. Like I accept the weather.

I felt the chill reaching my damp underwear, the discomfort I'd brought with me from the outside, and I wondered if her judgment wasn't a little cockeyed.

Perhaps it was because Philip was more like a friend and he seemed warmer to me.

"Don't do this, Ellen." Frank Butler looked disturbed and unhappy. "This isn't necessary."

I don't mind, Frank. Really, I don't. Mr. Hardman asked the question and he deserves an honest answer. She was stronger now. The misty look and some of the hurt was gone. *I believe I knew then. I suppose I didn't want to admit it to myself. This time the girl was important to him. It was important enough so that he lied beautifully for her. He used an imagination I didn't know he had. In time, I had to admit that it wasn't an infatuation. It didn't pass. I waited very patiently for some sign that it was over. Until I realized that I wasn't waiting for some sign that the affair was over but some indication that the marriage was over.* Her eyes were open, not blinking. *You know, in marriages, you see what you want to and you believe what you want to. It is hard to believe what is true, even when it is all around you.*

Frank Butler tried again. "Ellen, this isn't answering his question."

She ignored him. *Until today, I didn't know who the woman was. I thought it might be one of my friends. It usually is, you know. And now I don't know whether I'm supposed to be happy or not that it isn't. I guess I should.*

"Maybe I'd better back off," I said. "It's a hunch I got. I can't say for sure that it was this woman."

What's her name?

"Her name is Reggie... Regina."

That night, the night of the party, the girl said a friend had dropped her here. She wanted to call a cab to take her home when she'd finished work. That was after all the guests had left. I may even have insisted that Philip drive her home. At least I have a memory of that. It didn't seem important at the time. After all, sometimes he drove the cleaning woman home rather than have her wait at the bus stop. Of course, that was on rainy or especially cold days.

Odd. I began to realize that she was calling him Philip now. Before, it had been Philly. Maybe Frank Butler started it. His very proper and correct manner of speech. The old world manners.

But I didn't think that was what Ellen Chambers was doing. Ellen was wedging in the distance. The ice age was coming and that wasn't the way the Flames, the Atlanta hockey team, meant the slogan.

There was more. There was much more she had to say. I reached in deep in my gut, where the secret button is, and turned it off so that I could stop listening.

It was steam hot in the Ford. I opened all the windows and then I stood on the driver's side and tried to fan out the hot air by swinging the door in and out. I didn't know if it would work but it seemed worth a try.

"Mr. Hardman?"

I looked over the car roof and saw Frank Butler crossing the lawn toward me. His dark and conservative coat was unbuttoned, flapping like wings at his sides.

"Yes?"

He rounded the front of the car and stopped on the other side of the car door. "You're a strange man. You left without discussing your fee."

"It was too close in there for me," I said.

"I think I could agree with you." He turned and gave me his profile while he stared at the front of the house. "These matters are always sad and painful."

When he continued to stare in that direction, I shifted and placed a hand on the roof. It came away burned but I thought I saw the shift of the drapes on one side of the window. It could have been the air conditioned wind tunnel in there. Or it might be Ellen Chambers watching us.

"It's two hundred a day." I didn't feel like going into the spiel about how it had to be split with my partner. It was too long a story and I halfway hoped that he'd decide I was overpriced. All I wanted was to get as far away from the split level house as I could. I hated bad marriages and the ends of them, the pus and the rot that people cleaned out of the wounds.

Frank Butler didn't protest my tab.

"I take care of the small expenses," I said. "I put in for long trips and plane tickets and hotel rooms and items like that."

He nodded. The nod was abstracted. His eyes were still fixed on the front window of the house. His mind, it seemed, was on other matters. "I have to make one point clear with you, Mr. Hardman, before you can consider yourself hired by my firm or by Mrs. Chambers."

"What?"

"Philip Chambers is not, at this moment, guilty of any crime. He hasn't done anything for which he could be taken to court. In the matter of the securities that he borrowed on, Ellen is quite willing to say that this transaction was carried out with her approval. That is, she won't question the legality of the signature on any documents that are a part of that transaction."

"Easy on him," I said.

"It is, of course, her wish."

"Maybe you didn't follow my drift in there."

"I think I did," Frank Butler said.

"You're not acting like it," I said. "Look, I think Philly was involved in the robbing of his own safe. I think he set up the buy back of the jewelry so he could collect another fifty thousand in goodbye cash."

"It is no crime for a man to open his own safe." The heat didn't appear to bother him. He still looked cool and crisp. Didn't the rich sweat like everybody else? "Or to delegate that authority to someone while he is out of town."

"You going to argue it that way?"

"I'm not sure. I think I could."

I tossed another brick at him. "There's the claim against the insurance company. That could be fraud."

"I don't think it would go to trial. It could be worked out with the insurance company. If necessary, the claim could be dropped. I could arrange that over lunch one day this week."

He could. I knew that he could. It was the way those matters were handled downtown. A good lunch at one of the clubs. Perhaps an inside stock tip to the company president or vice-president. An "in" into some quick money deal. It wouldn't be offered as payment for anything. It was just the way the big boys talked. And then, somewhere between the meal and the coffee, there'd be talk about the wayward husband, the nice young man who'd fallen in with the wrong woman. The young man might go to jail if the situation couldn't be worked out. Of course, it could. Favor for favor. And, Butler'd say, you do know that Ellen

Chambers is the daughter of so and so. It would be settled. The claim dropped. The file cleared.

I felt crowded. Like somebody was sucking my breath. "Look, maybe you want somebody else for this job. You do and I'll back off. The proviso still holds."

A slight shake of his head. "For some reason Mrs. Chambers wants you."

Boxed. I dipped my head a time or two. That was the handshake.

"Locate Philip. Ellen and I will take over at that point."

"I'll find him. It might take a week. It might take two."

"I want a progress report every two days." He stuck a couple of fingers in his suit pocket and brought out a business card. "Do you know any other problems that I ought to consider?"

"None." In the sneaky part of my head I crossed my fingers. That was a lie. There was one more matter, the messy one that all the lunches at the club couldn't settle. The nasty fall. The hard-assed one. It concerned Bob Jaynes, the part time bartender they'd dug out of the abandoned well in the country. Barbara's husband.

"Fine. I believe that Ellen and I can convince him, once you've located him, that this affair is not in his best interest."

Butler had dodged the other bricks. The borrowed-on stock and the peeled safe. Given time, he could probably work some fairy tale out that would explain away the body. I didn't want to give him that advance warning. I'd store Jaynes away. It would keep in some dark pocket until I knew more.

Fanning the car door hadn't helped. It was still hot inside. I got in and kicked the engine over. When I looked back, I saw that Frank Butler had crossed the lawn and reached the front door. Ellen Chambers met him in the doorway. And then I turned a corner and trees beside the road blocked my view of them. Not that I could read lips. Not that I could hear at this distance.

Riches. Oh, those riches. Everybody wanted to hire me. The economy was picking up. First Barbara. Then George Vickers. Then Philly Chambers. Now Ellen Chambers and/or her lawyer.

It was fat times if your heart was lean enough. If you didn't care what you did for the money. I wasn't sure. I was still on the fence.

CHAPTER FOURTEEN

"What kind of pipe you been smoking? The little brass one with the wire mesh to hold the hash?"

"Not that kind," I said.

The shade had edge-walked its path across the backyard until the porch steps were half in shadow and half in the sun. I'd got there first and I'd staked out the shade part. Art Maloney was in the sun, blinking into the low slant of the harsh light. Hump was behind us, his back against the porch screen door. Both of them were drinking my beer and acting toward me like I'd just blown a cylinder in my head.

Art reached for my smokes. The pack was on the step between us. I got my hand there first and covered it. "You smoke those and you might start believing me."

"I'll take the risk."

I moved my hand. He shook out a Pall Mall and lit it with my lighter.

"And," he said, "you base all this on the fact that Philly Chambers took off for parts unknown last night?"

"Thin," Hump said behind me.

I looked over my shoulder at him. He shrugged. "That and the fact that he borrowed on the securities that were supposed to be stolen from the wall safe. Add to that the buy back of the jewelry. Nobody else who'd been robbed got approached."

Art blew a curl of smoke at me. "So, he took the securities out of the safe a few days before the break-in. He put them in his glove compartment and doesn't get around to taking them by the bank." Or to forging her signature on the loan form. I didn't bother to butt in. "And because he's a forgetful fellow, he forgets to tell anybody that the securities weren't in the safe when it was cracked. And as far as the buy back goes, maybe the Chambers jewelry was the only batch worth the risk and trouble."

"You believe all this, I've got a good bunch of Confederate money I'd like to sell you. Fifty cents on the dollar. It's a sure investment."

"And his wife's not bitching," Art said.

"That lady's got money she ain't counted yet. More money than brains. She's one of those hopeless women, the ones who love and forgive."

"Fine women, those," Hump said.

"I think Philly and the Reggie girl got involved," I said. "That was back in May or early June. Maybe it was close enough so that she could tell him what she was really doing bartending those parties. He probably didn't care. If the hook was in, he probably didn't care if she was living with whoever it is that runs the operation."

"Handsome and distinguished man with gray hair. Picks girls up in front of homes for business girls when they get thrown out."

I nodded at Hump. "Might be. So Philly and Reggie girl are thinking about bugging out. Only Philly don't have the kind of money they need. The cash belongs to his wife. The sort of living Philly and the girl want to do you can't afford on slices of bread. You need as much of the loaf as you can get. They start thinking about ways to get their hands on it. And there's that wall safe. Might be he could have opened it. And he could have cleaned it. Doing it might have made problems with his wife. How'd he know she'd lie and cover for him? But back to the plot. Could be they approached Red and the others in the organization. Could be Reggie did it. But that's about the time the wife decides to have a party. She gets Philly to call the bar help service. Now Reggie Tilson is not about to bartend this party. The wife might feel the vibes between her and Philly. So Bob Jaynes is handed the job. Now this is the part that I have to hum. I don't know why Jaynes ended up in the dry well in the country. But I'm getting ahead of myself. The day after the party, Philly and his wife go to the lake for some sailing. Red and maybe Reggie and lord knows who else crack the safe. Might be Jaynes is involved to this point. I'm humming again. Maybe he didn't like the split. Anyway, Philly comes back to town. He's all innocent. Hell, he was out of town. Could be they had a meet. The others got their share out of the cash. Philly got the securities and the jewelry. He hocks the securities. They get the idea of selling the junk back to his wife. And that's another fifty thousand for the honeymoon."

"Even if I bought it so far, why check out on his wife?" Art asked. "Why not let it get cold and then leave?"

"I think he got scared. I might have flushed him by bringing in George Vickers. Maybe he knew then it wasn't as easy as he thought."

"Why do the buy back at all?" Hump said.

"Before he set the buy back up, might be he's not ready to leave. He wants that innocent look. He's got me to handle the dirt for him. It looks better."

"I especially like the parts where you hum," Art said.

"He don't hum that well," Hump said. "I like the *mights,* the *maybes* and the *could bes.*"

"The part concerns me is the killing… Jaynes and Red. Robbery and fraud are not in my line," Art said. "And all you do is *de-de-dum* when you get to them."

"Philly and the girl can sing all the words."

"A duet?"

"Solos and duets," I said. I carried my empty can to the garbage cart. When I lifted the top, the stench hit me. The smell wasn't bad in the winter, just when the hot sun was out. I dropped my Bud can in and slammed the top on. "Hump, who do you know at the Terminal Cab Company?"

"A driver named Benny Hunt."

"Yesterday, about six-thirty, a cab picked Philly up at his house on Lenox. You know the number. The cab was supposed to take him to the airport. I don't think it did."

"It might take time. If I can reach Benny, he can find out which cab from the dispatcher." Hump went inside. I heard him make a beer stop at the refrigerator and then his heavy tread on the way to the bedroom and the phone.

"I think you're trying this out on me," Art said. He flipped the cigarette butt against the garbage cart. "It's got more holes than real Swiss cheese. But go ahead and tell me the rest of it while I get a second beer."

"That's all of it," I said.

"I'll have a road beer then."

Hump was on the phone when we walked past the bedroom door. I followed Art to the driveway. He popped the tab on his roady and tossed it at me and backed out of the drive.

That was fine. He'd heard me out and his head was working away at the holes. In a few days, when I knew more, I could sing the parts I'd had to hum. He'd know the rest of it.

His name was Bill Slip. He needed a shave and his hair was long and shaggy under a Braves ball cap. He wore tan twill trousers and a short sleeve work shirt. His beer belly lapped over his belt buckle and he moved as if he pointed with the belly.

"I'll take one if you've got a spare." He nodded at the Bud can I held.

Hump opened one for him. He drank most of it in one swallow.

"Your time's worth ten?" I asked.

He wiped the foam from his upper lip with the back of his hand. "Ten ought to do it."

"Benny Hunt tells Hump you picked up a man on Lenox Road yesterday about six-thirty."

"Philly Chambers," Slip said. "I knew him." He touched his ball cap. "I'm a fan. I saw him pitch a time or two."

"You take him to the airport?"

"Who said I did that?"

"That's what Philly told his wife," I said.

"That he was going to the airport?" Bill Slip laughed.

"That's right."

"He didn't go anywheres close to the airport."

I reached in my pocket and fingered out a ten. I placed it on the kitchen table. Bill Slip scooped it from the table with two fingers and inserted it in his shirt pocket.

"Am I going to get him in trouble with his wife? He seemed like a nice enough guy."

"Naw." I shook my head at him. "He and the wife had an argument. He left home. She's looking for him so she can talk him into coming home again."

"The truth is I dropped him in front of Brookwood Station."

"Any train leaving last night?"

"Not that I know of. That's what threw me. I told him he was a day or two early for the train to New Orleans."

"What'd he say?"

"He didn't say anything. He slapped me on the back and tipped me a buck and went into the station."

"He carrying much baggage?"

"A little leather handbag. What we used to call a satchel."

"That all of it?" I turned to Hump. He shook his head. He didn't have any questions.

Bill Slip thought the question was for him. "Well, I didn't stay around to see if he came out again."

"It would have been worth another ten if you had."

"Next time I'll do just that." Slip tipped back the beer can and gulped the foam. He looked around for the trash can, didn't see it and left the can on the table.

Hump walked out front with him. I dropped the beer can in the trash.

He hadn't been that much help.

"It occurs to me," Hump said, "that Brookwood Station was Philly's way of sweeping his footprints away."

"He knows his wife."

"That means?"

"Ellen Chambers bought herself a man and she ain't going to turn him loose anyway but for the grave."

"Harsh," Hump said. "Now you are being extremely harsh."

We were driving out Peachtree. After Bill Slip left, we'd decided on a look-about. Not that we thought we'd learn much from it. Call it an afternoon drive, a time to look at the girls, and maybe a chance to stop by one of the singles bars and see what kind of trim had moved to town in the last few weeks.

We passed Pershing Point. It's here that Peachtree and West Peachtree join and become Peachtree Road. Past the curve there it's only a couple of blocks to Brookwood Station.

Hump slowed when we reached the Station. Philly Chambers didn't walk out of the main door. So much for that. But I decided that we'd come this far through the afternoon traffic and we might as well pretend that we were working. "All right, Philly knows that she'll have people looking for him. He's got a day or two. That's before I put the pressure on about the thousand dollars and the tall tale about the trip to New York gets shown for what it is. So, he has the cab drop him at Brookwood. Why?"

"So he can check into the Riviera Motel. That's almost next door."

"I don't think so."

"So he can catch a cab," Hump said.

"Or a bus. Or he could walk."

"Walk where?"

"Maybe here." I pointed. We were passing the intersection of Peachtree and 26th. The front of the Blanchard apartment house looked dingy in the late afternoon light. George Vickers's man, Dave Cathay, had tailed the two men from the stadium. They'd led him here. And then he'd lost them.

Hump worked his way into the right-hand lane. He pulled off the street. We were behind the 7–11 store, as we'd been the night before when we'd met Dave Cathay.

Hump leaned forward, his elbows on the wheel and his head angled toward me. The question wrinkles were on his forehead.

"Say Dave Cathay read it wrong. Say he's young and nervous and he needs help on the trail that he doesn't get. In his head, he's running the film of some 1940 private eye who gets lured somewhere and beat up on. He's too scared to walk in there and find out where those two men went. So when they come out ten minutes later, he pats himself on the back for not being tricked. Man, he's smart. And then he loses them. He says to himself that it is safe to go to the Blanchard now. He talks to the resident manager. But he asks the wrong question. He asks about the two men. They don't live there. That information backs up what his fear had told him."

"What about us? Why'd we buy it?"

"Other matters get in the way. He's waving a piece at me. And we're mad because Vickers tricked us and because, having done that, they've lost the two men. All that crap mixed in, maybe we don't see the real facts."

"Which facts?"

"That Dave Cathay didn't know the right question to ask. He didn't ask if Philly Chambers and Reggie Tilson live there." I pointed across the street.

✤ ✤ ✤

We parked Hump's Buick on 26th with the nose pointed toward Peachtree. The main entrance into the apartment building was on the 26th Street side and there was a parking lot in back for residents. Peachtree didn't have a tree showing. On 26th, the street was lined with old trees and we were in the shadow and shade of what must have been a hundred-year-old oak.

At twilight, the people traffic was heavy. Mostly going into the building. Working girls with the bounce gone out of their walk. Old ladies with their grocery bags clutched in one hand and the dog leash in the other. The single studs in their best clothes, striding with the stutter-step that the afternoon drinks put in their walk.

And then it slowed. It was suppertime all over Atlanta. Suddenly, before we knew it, it was dark. Peachtree, with the lamps on, looked like a river of fire. 26th Street, with its preserved trees, had few lamps. I liked it that way. Maybe we wouldn't be noticed.

Nine o'clock.

Nine-thirty. Hump said, "I don't feel like wasting the rest of the night on this. One thing to stay here when you know for sure somebody's in there, but when it's only a wild guess…"

I touched his arm. A blonde girl came out of the apartment building. She stopped just outside the door. The full light from overhead struck her. She wore white tight-fitting slacks and a print blouse.

"Could be," I said.

"Lot of blondes in town that ain't named Tilson."

No way to argue with him. And then we had luck. Philly Chambers stepped through the doorway and stood facing her on the walk. We couldn't hear them. From the way they gestured it appeared they were having an argument. The girl insisted this.

He insisted that. Finally, he shrugged and gave up. He spun about and marched back into the apartment house.

I had to say it fast. I didn't know how much time I had. "If she gets in a car, soon as she's in, you get out. You check the apartment house. Find where they're staying. Run any con you have to. When you've done that, walk down to Clarence Foster's. Wait at the bar. Either I'll come by or I'll call."

The blonde girl remained on the far side of the street. She headed toward Peachtree.

Hump put his hand on the door handle. "I could go ahead and take him. I could be waiting for you."

I shook my head. "That's not what the job calls for."

The girl angled across the street. A battered old gray Volvo was parked there. While she bent over the lock I said, "Go ahead," and blinked at the brief flash of overhead light while the car door was open. Then he was on the sidewalk and I slid behind the wheel.

The traffic light at Peachtree was red. I watched the Volvo edge toward the intersection. I started the Buick's engine but didn't hit the headlights. When the traffic light changed, I waited until she'd made her right turn before I eased away from the curb.

It was a straight shot down Peachtree Road. Then down West Peachtree. A right just past the Sheraton-Biltmore onto 5th. Down 5th to Argonne. A left on Argonne where it dead-ended.

I laid back. I let the rope stay loose.

Down Argonne to 8th where she took a right. A straight line down 8th, headed toward the Grady High School block. Didn't quite reach it. A right on Charles Allen. I made the turn and saw, just in time, that the Volvo had pulled to the curb half a block down Charles Allen. I was too close to stop. I went by. Down two blocks until I could make my turn out of sight, on the left around a grass-centered triangle. Back on Charles Allen. Taking it slow. From half a block away, I got a white flash of her crossing the street. A blur of her white slacks.

I cut my headlights and nudged the curb. I was close enough so that she might have noticed me. She didn't. Another car roared past me from behind and locked her in the lights.

The girl reached the narrow porch of what looked like a renovated townhouse. The porch light was on. I saw her reach for the knocker and give the door a couple of raps. After about a minute, the door opened and a man stood in the lighted doorway. A handsome man in his forties. A man with gray hair. Well dressed. Not wearing a suit coat now but still with a tie and a buttoned vest.

The man put an arm around the blonde girl's shoulder and walked her through the doorway. The door slammed behind them.

It was forty-five minutes before she came out again. Now she carried a make-up or overnight case. The same man was with her. He carried two large suitcases. They crossed the street. The girl opened the car door and the man put the suitcases inside. The girl leaned past him and added the case she carried.

Moving on, I said. It is moving on time.

And then, while I watched from the darkness of the Buick, they kissed like movie stars. The kiss and grope lasted about five minutes. It was, I decided, the goodbye and maybe I'll never see you again kind of kiss.

CHAPTER FIFTEEN

The Volvo moved into the turn lane at 26th Street. I remained where I was. I saw the Volvo taillights wink at me as I passed. A couple of blocks beyond that intersection I pulled into the Clarence Foster's drive and stopped, blocking it. As soon as I opened the barroom door, Hump saw me and pushed his drink away.

Out at the driveway, two cars were stacked behind us. Hump got behind the wheel. We looped the back parking lot and reached Peachtree Road again.

"Tell me," I said.

"Second floor. Apartment 2D. In the name of Philip Kane and his wife, Ruth."

"They got the right sounds to the first names anyway."

"All those beginners see too many crime movies," Hump said.

We caught the red light at 26th. I said I had to make a couple of calls. "Keep a good watch. I think they're getting ready to move."

I dodged traffic. I got caught in the light change when I was halfway across the street. A fast-moving VW tried to wipe his left front fender on me. I sucked it in like I'd seen a bullfighter do once and made the other sidewalk.

I found a pay phone in the 7–11 store. I placed the first call to Art Maloney at the Police Department. I told him that we'd located Philly and the girl and that I thought the man at Robbery might be interested in the people at the townhouse on Charles Allen Drive.

"Betts," Art said. "I'll pass the word."

"Is that all?" I leaned a shoulder against the wall and watched the store clerk pick his nose. He did it like he didn't know what his finger was doing. "Don't you want to talk to Reggie Tilson?"

"If she'd talk. I just don't know what charge I could put on her."

There was truth in that. I didn't know either. "Let me get back to you. I've got another call to make."

"How soon?"

"Five minutes."

"I'll wait." He hung up.

I dialed Ellen Chambers. She answered on the second ring. "I've found Philly."

"Already? Why, that's wonderful, Mr. Hardman."

I agreed with her that it was. "There's a minor problem. I've got a feeling they're getting ready to move on." I wouldn't swear to that guess and I wouldn't bet on it. Might be Philly and the girl were settling in for the honeymoon on Peachtree and 26th. But I was thinking sneaky. It wouldn't hurt to let Ellen Chambers think she had a deadline. It had been a long day and it was time to get this crappy business done with.

"I'll call Frank Butler. I know he'll come with me. But it might be an hour before we get there."

"Soon as you can," I said.

"How will we find you?"

"Pull onto 26th and park as close to Peachtree as you can. We'll find you."

I broke the connection and dialed Art again. While the phone rang, I checked the clock on the store wall. It was ten of eleven.

"Yeah?"

"Do what you want to," I said, "but there is going to be a ruckus in 2D of the Blanchard Apartments around midnight. Might be you'd want to drop by."

"And just knock on the door?"

"Come early and go as my guest. Come late and knock on the door and I'll let you in."

"Do I have to do the secret knock?"

He was laughing when I hung up on him.

I bought four packaged sandwiches and a six pack of beer. Hump lifted his head from the steering wheel when I eased into the Buick's passenger seat. "How's it going?" I passed him two sandwiches and a Bud.

He ate the first sandwich in two bites. He washed the clot down with a swallow of beer. "I think you're right about them moving on."

"How do you know?"

"Two or three minutes ago, Philly put two suitcases in the red and gray Coupe de Ville. It's parked in the back lot there. He spent some time arranging the trunk. I think the girl must have put hers in right after she got here from Charles Allen."

"I wouldn't want them to leave before midnight. I think we're going to witness a domestic dispute of earthquake dimensions."

"And kicking and screaming too?"

"That too."

Hump shoved half of his second sandwich in his mouth and leaned across me. He hit the lock on the glove compartment. He fumbled a few seconds before he said, "Yeah," and backed away. I heard a click and saw that he had a switchblade with a six-inch blade in his cupped hand. He chewed for a few seconds and cleared his throat. "Watch my back."

I said I would.

I watched him stroll across the street. He seemed to glide over the parking lot surface. The Coupe de Ville was in one of the slots near the street. He patted its trunk the way you'd pat a dog. He took his slow look around. He ducked and went out of sight. I knew he'd moved toward the left front tire. A couple of seconds and he appeared once more. A slow stroll across the street and he got behind the wheel. I passed him his can of beer. He passed me the closed switchblade. I tossed it in the glove compartment and closed it.

"He ain't going anywhere."

"What kind of trouble's he got?"

"Flat left front tire. Dead flat. You know how long it takes to get a service station to send a truck over this time of night? Just about forever. And I don't see Philly getting his hands dirty changing the tire."

At five of midnight, a black Continental pulled into 26th Street and parked on the road fifty feet from us. Frank Butler got out and stood in the street next to the Continental. I walked down to meet him.

Frank Butler planted his feet squarely in front of the door to apartment 2D. Small and dapper, he looked like James Cagney about to start a tapdance. I was a few feet away, down the hall with Ellen Chambers. Hump had flattened himself against the wall to the right of the door.

Butler hit the doorbell for the second time. He held the button in for a count of thirty. I could, from the side, see his lips tick off the slow numbers.

He jerked his hand away when the lock snicked and the door opened a few inches. Philly Chambers stood in the doorway. He was bare-chested and wearing only pajama bottoms. It was a blank sleepy look he gave Frank Butler.

"I think we have to talk," Butler said.

"Frank, we don't have anything to talk about."

Behind Philly, from about a room's distance away we heard the woman's voice. "If that is Burt you tell him to go away. I said all I wanted to say to him earlier tonight."

Philly didn't bother to answer her. "Go away, Frank. Tell Ellen to forget…"

He was edging the door forward, closing it. Butler looked over his shoulder at Hump. That was the cue. Hump swung away from the wall. His hands were out and he hit the door with both palms. Philly said, "What the hell...?" and grabbed the door. Hump rammed his shoulder with all that weight behind it. The door hit Philly in the chest and knocked him back.

Frank Butler stepped through the doorway. Hump was in lockstep with him. I turned to take Ellen Chambers by the elbow. She wasn't there. She was sprinting down the hall. I ran after her. I reached the doorway a step behind her. Philly Chambers was on his rump on the carpet. He said, "Goddam you..." and reached back to push himself to his feet. He didn't make it. Ellen let out a yell somewhere between a choked name call and a squeal and launched herself at him. He couldn't get his hands up in time. She landed on him and the wind grunted out of him. I think I heard them butt heads. Even with the head knock and the wind gone, he tried to push her away. He couldn't. She had the weight and the width on him.

I stepped into the apartment. I reached behind me and slammed the hallway door. I backed against the door and, with an arm behind me, I twisted the lock and heard it slide into place.

I couldn't take my eyes off the struggle on the carpet. It was funny and sad at the same time. Watching them writhe, hearing them grunt and hiss, I had an inside feeling that I knew what it was like to be in the same lusty bed with her. It bothered Butler too. He said, "Ellen... Ellen." He waved an arm at Hump. A couple of steps and Hump bent over them. He caught Ellen Chambers by the arms and pulled her away. He stood her on her feet and drew her to the side.

Philly sat up. Both hands came up and rubbed his forehead. I guess that was where she'd butted him.

"Philly... what... who...?"

Reggie Tilson was in the bedroom doorway.

There was strong light behind her. She wore a sheer shortie nightgown. I got my eyes full of silky pubic hair and thick, finger-like, purple nipples on small breasts.

"Who the hell are you?"

"Marriage doctors on a house call," I said.

Philly looked over his shoulder and saw what I saw. "Don't stand there. Put on some clothes."

She didn't take orders well. She stared at the huge, disarrayed shape of Ellen Chambers. "Is that the cow?"

"Cow? You call me a cow?" Ellen jerked one arm free and lunged for the girl. Hump recovered and wrapped both arms around Ellen's waist and pulled her away.

"Reggie, dammit, shut up." Philly said.

The girl whirled out of the doorway and slammed the bed-room door shut. Philly got to his knees and then to his feet. He stood there, swaying from side to side. "What is this supposed to be, Frank?"

"I said we've got to talk, Philip." Butler was turning slowly on his heels, having his look around the living room.

"We don't have anything to talk about."

Butler selected his chair. It was the big stuffed easy chair to the left of the sofa. He moved in that direction and eased himself into the deep seat cushion. "I assure you, Philip, that I didn't come all the way over here at this hour of the night *not* to have a talk." He was calm. The ice cold surface that nothing could chip or ruffle. "You sit there," he said.

He'd pointed at the end of the sofa near the easy chair. Philly acted like he had to sit down somewhere and it might as well be the seat that Butler had chosen for him. He settled onto the sofa and put his face in his hands.

"You sit there, Ellen." Frank Butler wagged a manicured fin-ger at the chair at the other end of the sofa. It was close enough so she'd feel a part of the talk but far away enough so that she could be stopped if she decided to make another grab for Philly.

Hump released Ellen. I watched in something like amazement at the graceful way she took her seat. The composed lady again after the brawling action a couple of minutes before.

Hump took a position behind Ellen's chair. I did a curl and put my back to the hallway door.

The stage was set. Frank Butler cleared his throat and began. "I think we are here tonight, Philip, to decide your future."

Philly lifted his face from his hands. "I want you to leave. All of you."

"I was a young man myself once," Butler said. "I understand what the temptations of the flesh can do to a man."

I flinched. It was a bit overripe even for a courtroom. In a living room after midnight it was a clinker.

"You were never young," Philly said. "You were born forty years old."

It was water off Butler's back. He didn't appear to hear Philly. It was as if he'd paused for effect, to let the silence work for him. And then he went into high gear. It was the most beautiful summation I've heard and I've been in court a few times.

Butler talked about prison. It was hell on earth. It was bread and rusty water and food a pig wouldn't eat. And don't you believe what you hear about those country club prisons where the rich go. Everybody didn't get in those. The prison he was talking about was hard time and no comforts and no booze and no women. And some men got so lonely they started liking other men. That was shocking.

About the time Philly must have felt like asking why Butler was going to all that trouble to describe prisons to him, Frank shifted gears one more time. He was talking, in a calm and reasonable voice, about those crimes against society that landed a young man in prison. There was, for example, forgery and fraud committed against a bank when you borrowed against securities that you didn't entirely own. Of course, someone like a wife might not want to testify that the signature on the transaction papers wasn't hers. But a skillful prosecutor could force her to tell the truth. And there was the kind of fraud involved in false claims placed against an insurance company. Insurance companies were notorious for wanting to make examples out of people who attempted fraud against them.

And a big part of getting justice in the courts was having a good lawyer to defend you. Often a young man who didn't have his wife's financial backing didn't have funds and he had to settle for a public defender. He'd probably be some young man just out of law school who'd never been in court before.

It was beautiful. It had a design. It was so good that Ellen started sniffling with the prison part. She was choking back sobs when Butler reached the section about the inexperienced lawyer.

Philly looked shocked and stunned.

I got so involved in the summation that I couldn't help joining in. "How long do you think this man would get, Mr. Butler?"

"On the two charges, if he were found guilty, I'd say a minimum of ten years." He didn't look at me. He was giving Philly his Uncle Frank stare. But I could tell from the way he answered that I'd made him happy.

Reggie Tilson came from the bedroom. She'd dressed in the same white slacks and the print blouse she'd been wearing earlier in the night. The way her small breasts jiggled, I knew that she hadn't gone to the trouble to look for a bra.

It was a good entrance. I felt a bit of a growl in my groin and I saw the hawk look Hump gave her. It was wasted on Philly. Frank Butler had the three-pronged hook in his hide.

Reggie threw back her shoulder and pointed the purple nipples at Philly. "Tell these people to leave, Philly."

Philly didn't turn his head. He said, "Shut up."

I knew it was over then. At least half over. Frank Butler had laid out the worst of it. All that was left was to tell the young man what his good options were.

Before the oiled gears shifted once more, there was a knock at the door. It was the secret knock we kidded about. I could almost see him smiling. Two raps close together, a pause while he counted to five, and three more taps close together.

I opened the door before anyone could tell me not to.

Art walked in and gave me a sour look. It was his way of protecting me as a source. "You're here? I guess we got here the same way."

"The taxi driver," I said.

He nodded. He reached into his jacket pocket and brought out his I.D. and his badge. "Atlanta Police," he said.

We couldn't have timed it better or staged it better if we'd huddled over lunch and assigned the roles and established the entrance cues.

What we had was a play called *The Wayward Husband* or *Crime Pays Very Well, Except in Apartment 2D*. It's a farce and this detective walks in at the right moment and flashes his badge. The wayward husband is weakening and the *other* woman knows it and she's ready to make her pitch for his love and loyalty. The air goes out of it when he says, "Atlanta Police," and he looks at the *other* woman with a hard eye and he says, "You're Regina Tilson and I want to talk to you downtown about two murders."

Oh, lordy, look at the wayward husband. He looks like he's going to be sick on the rug. You can almost see him pulling away from Reggie Tilson and leaning toward the soft uncle shoulder that Frank Butler is offering him. And he's thinking about all that legal knowledge that Butler has stored away.

The wronged wife has stopped sniffling and sobbing. She's staring at the wayward husband with a buyer's eye. She knows the price tag and she knows what's in her purse and she's looking at the *other* woman the way she looks at last year's dingy underwear.

And the wayward husband knows that the wronged wife, in a few days, in a week, after she has made him suffer enough, will allow him in her bed and he will have to make magnificent love to her. She will expect it of him. And he knows that his eyes will be closed and his mind will be filled with the color pictures of younger women, of hard rumps and silk hair and oil slick mouths. And he knows he will have to do his multiplication tables in his head so he won't lose it, so that he will last until she screams that she is satisfied.

It wasn't exactly that farce. Not exactly.

While the others stared at Art, and he introduced himself to Reggie Tilson, I slipped into the bedroom and closed the door behind me. The bed looked like an army had marched through it. The closet was empty except for a shirt, trousers and a jacket that belonged to Philly.

On the chair next to the bed, I found the leather briefcase. It wasn't locked so I had my look. It was a feast for poor eyes. Stacks and stacks of money. All with the bank bands still on. I lifted the case and estimated the weight. Pounds and pounds. And thinking back over the deals that Philly had pulled in the last week I guessed that it was somewhere between a hundred and two hundred thousand dollars.

I bent over the open briefcase. I read the faces of the bills that were on top. What interested me were the serial numbers. Finally, I selected one banded stack. I took it out and closed the briefcase. I carried the case into the living room.

I had to wait to do my scene. Art was doing his. He was saying, "…Betts is at the townhouse on Charles Allen with a search warrant at this minute. If he finds any stolen goods there, then the fat is in the fire."

Reggie lifted her chin and said, "I don't know anyone who lives on Charles Allen."

Art looked past her at me.

"That's a lie. I followed you there," I said. "You were inside the house for forty-five minutes. When you came out, you were carrying a make-up or vanity case. The man with you was carrying two suitcases for you. I wrote the times down and I'll swear to it in court."

"You might have to," Art said.

Reggie Tilson drew her lips together in a tight line and locked her teeth.

I waited, and when there was silence, I knew I could do my scene. I lifted the briefcase of money. "I found this in the bedroom."

Reggie jumped for me. I threw the case over her toward Art. He caught it. Reggie fell thigh-to-thigh against me and I had to push a claw hand away from my face.

"And something else. This is part of the fifty thousand I turned over to that dude at the stadium in the buy back." I waved the banded stack of money.

Art could be the straight man when he had to. "What makes you sure? Could you swear to it in court?"

"No doubt about it. I had to run through the money so I could sign a receipt Mrs. Chambers wanted." I nodded at Ellen. "This one twenty on top of one of the stacks grabbed me. I was looking at it as if I had that bill in a game of Liars Poker." I looked at the bill. "Trip nines to start with, two zeros that count as tens, another nine and two more tens. I remember thinking to myself that with four nines and four tens I could do myself some lying."

Art reached for the banded stack of bills. He had the briefcase tucked under one arm. He pulled a pen from his pocket and said, "I'll mark this as evidence." He scribbled on the bank band.

Then he opened the briefcase and placed the stack inside with the others.

"Where's the phone?"

I waved Art toward the bedroom. It was so quiet in the living room that everybody heard him order a paddy wagon. From my position, I watched Reggie Tilson's face. I didn't see any reaction at all. I think she'd expected it.

On his way back into the living room Art touched Reggie on the shoulder. "You're going to have to come along with me." He waved two fingers at me and I fished out my smokes and passed them to him. When he had a cigarette going, he tilted his head at Philly. "You too, Mr. Chambers."

Philly flinched. He appealed to Butler. "Can he do this?"

"For a time," Frank Butler said. "Of course, if I were your attorney of record ..."

"Would you?"

That sauced the duck. Philly had jumped off the wall. I knew it and everybody in the room knew it. Reggie Tilson waited her time before she showed how she felt about it. When Philly passed her on the way to the bedroom, to dress before the wagon arrived, Reggie reached out a hand and clawed him down the right side of his face. She hissed, "Scum" at him.

The wagon drove in ten minutes later.

Hump and I did a couple of bars.

It was twenty after four when Hump dropped me in front of my house. I got as far as the bedroom door before the scent of the Charlie perfume hit me about nose high. I didn't bother with the light. I sat on the edge of the bed and kicked off my shoes. I threw my clothes across the room and heard change rolling in all directions.

Marcy didn't move. I thought she was awake.

I said, "I think somebody has been sleeping in my bed."

"I came to return your key and you weren't here."

"I didn't see your car."

"I took a cab," she said.

"That tricky ploy, huh?"

Marcy said, "Shut up, Jim, and come over here."

I did.

CHAPTER SIXTEEN

I got through Wednesday. I slept until two in the afternoon and Marcy called in sick. Somewhere in there we talked about the trip to the mountains. It was set for late Friday, an hour or so after Marcy got off work.

Art looked in on me on Thursday. I'd been interested but I hadn't called. I wanted the straight word after all the loose ends had been tied together.

The wayward husband and the *other* woman weren't getting along well. In fact, after Hump and I had left, they'd had a bit of a fight in the paddy wagon. She'd wanted to relieve him of one of his eyes and he'd broken two of her fingers defending himself.

With the advice and consent of Frank Butler, Philly was cooperating with the police. The way Art told it, Philly was shading everything a few notches in his favor. Maybe that was good coaching from Butler. And the faithful, long suffering wife was at the jail as often as they'd allow the visits. That was often.

"You had the big parts of it right," Art said.

"That's gratifying."

"Of course, there was the place you had to hum."

"The Bob Jaynes killing?"

"It goes like this. The gray-haired dude from Charles Allen Drive, his name is Burt. He got caught with some of the stolen goods right in his house and he decides to tell us most of what he knows. He says that Red did the killing. You see, since this robbery at the Chambers house was an inside job, they didn't need a bartender for the casing or key stealing. The party that night was just bad timing by Ellen Chambers. Philly and Reggie had made their deal with Burt and Red. The ready cash in the safe was their share of the take. Reggie and Philly got the securities and the jewelry. But Bob Jaynes had been involved in casing one other job and he liked that extra money. So he balked at being left out. He worked the party that night and as far as he was concerned, that meant he ought to have a part of the split. His mouth was talking like it might have hinges and he might know the police department telephone number. Red took him off for a drink and some talk and a chance to cool off. When Red came back a couple of hours later, Bob Jaynes wasn't with him. He wouldn't say where Bob was. All he'd say was that they didn't have a problem anymore. Everybody ate any other questions they had. I think they were a little afraid of Red. They might have had reason. Burt gave us another name Red used to be known by. We're checking it now. Might be he was wanted up in Maryland."

We were in my backyard. We walked up the slope to the wall that fronts the terrace garden. I sat on the wall and blinked at the sun. Art leaned a hip against the wall and picked at some weed or other. The sky was clouding, getting darker.

"I hummed Red's killing too."

"Funny thing about that explosion," Art said. "Nobody seems to know beans about it. Burt and his two boys were playing poker together that night and they remember how surprised they were to hear what happened to Red."

"His two boys? Either of them match the one I saw planting the charge?"

Art shook his head. "Had to be an outsider. A freelancer."

"It's got to be tied in."

"Proof's the hard matter."

"Burt's two boys, they handle the stadium buy back Monday night?"

"Looks like it. It was easy money. An extra. A thousand each. When Philly and Reggie decided to do the buy back, they took the idea to Burt. He offered his boys."

Dark clouds obscured the sun. It might rain.

I had one more question. "How's Philly going to come out of this?"

"Pure as the driven slush."

"That's what cooperating does for you," I said.

"When Philly gets on the stand, he's so willing that he'll do everything but drop his trousers and moon the jury."

It was hot and bright Friday morning.

At ten that morning, I put in a call to the caretaker in Blowing Rock. That was the drill. By Friday, he'd know if anybody planned to use the house in Mayfair Manors. He remembered me and he said, no, it wasn't being used and he'd meet me at the Antlers Bar about ten that evening and I could buy him a few beers and he'd deliver the key to me.

I called Marcy at the office and gave her that news. It relaxed her some. We were going to the mountains anyway, whatever happened with the house in Mayfair Manor. But Marcy wasn't liberated enough to feel comfortable checking into motels with me.

I packed a bag and placed it next to the front door. I stood in the open doorway and considered a drive to the nearest beer store. I needed a case of Bud. Or if I wanted to be fancy, a case of Beck's. The beer laws in the mountains of North Carolina are strange. The last time I'd stayed in the house in Blowing Rock, they'd sold cold beer to drink in the bars but only warm beer to go.

So maybe I'd pack a cooler. Beer and a few steaks and perhaps a couple of pounds of green shrimp and a bottle or two of wine.

I leaned on the doorframe and looked out at my Ford. Now or later? Now or on the way out of town? And then the black Mercedes sedan pulled into my drive and parked behind my car. There. The decision had been made for me.

Ellen Chambers got out of the Mercedes. She was wearing a blue linen dress that barely reached her knees. The dress was high necked and it had embroidery around the yoke that looked like a wreath of small white flowers. She was bare legged and wore delicate white sandals. You could say one thing for her. She was fat and she didn't try to hide it in yards and yards of pant suit.

She stopped at the bottom of the steps and smiled at me. "I'm on my way to see Philly and I remembered that I still owed you for the day you spent looking for him."

I'd written that off. I'd wrapped that in the thousand dollars I'd gotten from Frank Butler. "It's not necessary. But if it bothers you, you can send me a check for two hundred and we'll call it even."

"I will."

I realized that she was waiting for me to ask her in. It wasn't going to be that short of a visit. So I asked her if she'd like some coffee. She said she didn't but the question got her through the doorway and into my living room.

"You don't mind, I'll have one," I said.

She followed me into the kitchen. The water in the kettle was still hot. I mixed myself a cup. When I turned, she was standing in the doorway. It was a tight squeeze. She almost served as a door.

"How is it with Philly?"

It wasn't that I really cared. Still, once you start playing the host, you have to make the small talk too.

"Frank thinks he'll get off with a year or two of probation."

"First offense?"

"That's a part of it." She nodded. "Frank thinks, with an understanding judge, probation is possible with these special circumstances."

If anybody could find an understanding judge, it would be Frank Butler. He'd been drinking and fishing and hunting with most of the judges in his time. All he needed to do was say the right key words, the shorthand, and the judge would be very understanding. The judge might give Philly a harsh lecture in court and Philly might have to sweat a few minutes. But he'd be free and probation for the rich was a very, very loose leash.

"Frank's trying to arrange bail today."

I sipped my coffee. "I'd say his chances are good."

And I thought about the leash. Probation wasn't just a threat the court could hold over Philly. It was a weapon they put in Ellen Chambers's hands too. And I had a feeling that if she got her wish it would be a long, long probational period.

"I don't know why it matters, Mr. Hardman."

Uh-uh. I could feel it coming.

"I really don't," she said, "but I have the feeling you don't approve of me ... of us."

"It shouldn't matter." I said it soft and easy. I left the snot out.

"It does."

"You don't need this. You've got Frank Butler. He gives the best advice in the whole town."

"It matters."

I shook my head.

"You might have to testify in court," she said.

"I'll stick to the facts."

"I'd still like to know."

"Shit." It exploded, the frustration and the anger. "I'm no Ann Landers. If I was, I'd say you ought to dump him. He's not worth the grief."

"You're very blunt, Mr. Hardman."

I shook my head slowly. "Why not?"

It didn't come out sounding right. I'd meant why shouldn't I be blunt. Maybe the anger messed up the inflection. Or maybe she really wasn't listening. She took it the other way. As if I'd questioned her, asked her why she shouldn't dump Philly out with the garbage.

"Because I love him," she said.

I backed away. It wasn't something we could argue. It wasn't logic or reason anymore. "I guess that's reason enough."

Then she threw the high school bit at me. That famous movie line. "You'd understand, Mr. Hardman, if you've ever been in love."

I sweated and blushed for her. She didn't notice. "You might be right," I said. And I thought about Marcy. Sometimes I thought I loved her. But there was an edge, a mark, I couldn't cross. If I crossed it, it was as much sickness as love. Instead of whole people, it would be cripples loving cripples and that was a disease.

I put down my cup and walked her to the door. I knew that she wasn't completely satisfied. And I believed I knew why she'd come to see me. She'd opened herself too much to me, that afternoon at her house. She'd hung some of her guts around her neck and now she felt she needed to justify herself.

All right. Trash up my house with your old leftover emotions.

"I'll mail the check," she said at the bottom of the steps.

I said that would be fine.

I watched her drive away.

It rained early that Saturday morning. We were under one of the homemade quilts that came with the house. Marcy was warm and bubbling away in her sleep. It was a gentle rain, the tapping of a drummer's brush.

Tell me who you love, Jim Hardman.

I couldn't answer my own question. Maybe there wasn't an answer. Perhaps it was a wine hangover dumb question. Or I didn't want to answer. I was afraid of what I'd say. And I knew about the hooks that came with love.

When I awoke again, it was first light and the mist was rising from the valley below and I stood at the window and watched it until it blotted out the mountains.

AFTERWORD

My Expensive Addiction
By Lee Goldberg

My expensive, life-changing addiction began six years ago when a man approached me in a nameless hotel in a city I don't remember.

"You're really going love this," Bill Crider said, almost in a whisper. "And I'm not going to let you leave here until you buy it."

We were standing in front of a used bookseller's table at a writer's conference. I looked down and saw that Bill was holding a yellowed, brittle paperback out to me. It was entitled *Hardman #1, The Charleston Knife is Back in Town* by Ralph Dennis. The slug line across the top of the cover read "Brace yourself for broads, bullets, and bare-fisted action!"

It was obvious from the numbered title that it was one of those cheap, men's action adventure paperbacks, a genre I knew well, having written, under the pseudonym "Ian Ludlow," a series called *.357 Vigilante* in the mid-1980s for the same publisher that released this book. While there were some gems in the genre, most of them were hack work, badly written excuses for explicit sex and graphic violence that were sold in grocery store spinner racks nationwide. And a book called "Hardman"— *wink, wink, nudge nudge*—promised to be among the worst of them.

Bill must have seen the skepticism on my face so he smiled and said, "Trust me. You won't regret it."

This is how it often is with pushers. *Have a taste,* they say, *it won't hurt you.*

And Bill was particularly good at pushing old paperbacks and forgotten authors. He was a kind, decent, warm man, an acclaimed author, and an expert on crime fiction. People trusted him. I trusted him.

So I bought the book...and quickly read it.

To my surprise, and delight, it was nothing like what I expected. Jim Hardman is in his 40s, a pudgy, balding ex-cop with a steady girlfriend...who does odd jobs with his drinking buddy Hump Evans, a black ex-NFL player who supports his playboy lifestyle by hiring himself out as muscle. They are functioning alcoholics, drinking booze morning, noon and night as if its mineral water, doing whatever they have to do, short of murder or bank robbery, to make a living in the seamy underworld of 1970s Atlanta, as equal partners and, although it remains unspoken, close friends.

This wasn't men's action-adventure fiction. This was straight-up, hardboiled crime fiction, written in a tight, evocative voice. And it was wonderful. I was so excited about what I was reading, I didn't even wait to finish the book before I raved to my friends about it on Facebook on November 20, 2012:

I am mid-way through what is labeled as Hardman #1: The Charleston Knife is Back in Town by Ralph Dennis (Pinnacle 1982)...but it's actually a reprint of book #2 in the series from 1974. No matter, I am loving it. So much so, that I've hunted down and ordered the rest of the books in the long out-of-print series, including the actual Hardman #1, Atlanta Deathwatch.

A few days later, I posted the one and only review at the time for *Charleston Knife* on Amazon:

Fantastic Series, Deserves Wide Acclaim.
   November 25, 2012
   Format: Mass Market Paperback
   It's a tragedy this book was marketed/packaged as a men's action adventure novel. Dennis was the real deal…these deserved to be recognized as straight-up noir. These novels pre-date Robert B. Parker's SPENSER series and yet are strikingly similar…Makes me wonder if Parker might have read one of the Hardmans at some point and it was percolating in his subconscious when he created his own series. Like Spenser, Hardman is an ex-cop turned investigator/bodyguard who lives by his own moral code and teams up often with a rough, violent African-American enforcer. He's also got a steady, loving girlfriend who understands, if not totally accepts, who he is and what he does (and isn't nearly as irritating as Susan Silverman), and a friend on the force (ala Belson and Quirk) who helps him out. He's also deeply tied in with the local mob bosses who have an understanding with him (again, like Spenser). And Atlanta, the city where Hardman lives, is a vivid character in the books (like Boston in the Spensers). The tone of the Hardmans is very different than the Spensers, and Spenser is far more moralistic, physically capable, smart-assy, and sure of himself than Hardman, but otherwise the franchise elements are almost identical. Ralph Dennis has a great voice, a wicked sense of humor, and a very sharp eye for detail. It's a damn shame this man never broke out into the big leagues. I loved this book and I am eager to devour the rest of this series.

That was an understatement. I set the rest of my life aside and quickly tore through the series, sharing my experience on social media as I went along. For example:

Facebook Status Update. December 3, 2012
Reading HARDMAN #3 by Ralph Dennis and am loving it.
What a great @#$%^ series. Tragedy it's so unknown and over-
looked. The rest of the books just arrived from booksellers across
the country. Can't wait to plow through'em all.

I was hooked. I had no idea how deeply.

As I was devouring the series, I started looking into Ralph
Dennis. There was very little written about him. I learned that
he was born in 1931 in Sumter, South Carolina and received a
Masters degree from University of North Carolina, where he
later taught film and television writing after serving a stint in
the Navy.

Atlanta Deathwatch was the first novel he sold … and he
wrote the next six novels in the *Hardman* series in just one
year. That amazed me. There was a time when I was writing four books a year, alternating between original *Diagnosis
Murder* and *Monk* novels, and it nearly killed me.

The first seven *Hardman* novels were published in rapid suc-
cession by Popular Library in 1974 and were poorly packaged as a
cheap men's action-adventure paperbacks with numbered titles.

Even so, and this is truly astonishing, somehow some top
critics got their hands on the books and saw past the cheesy
covers. The *New York Times* praised the *Hardman* novels for
"expert writing, plotting, and an unusual degree of sensitiv-
ity. Dennis has mastered the genre and supplied top entertain-
ment." The *Philadelphia Daily News* proclaimed *Hardman* "the
best series around, but they've got such terrible covers…"
Unfortunately, Popular Library didn't take the hint and continued to present the series as numbered hack work, dooming the
novels to a short shelf-life and obscurity.

Ralph Dennis wanted more... and deserved better. So he walked away from the series, trying his luck with a paperback potboiler (*Atlanta*, Popular Library 1975) and the first book in what he hoped would be a harder-edged series (*Dead Man's Game*, Berkley 1976). But when both books bombed, he returned to *Hardman*, writing six more in the series that Popular Library released between 1976 and 1977.

His final, published novel was his shot at the big time: a hard-cover, World War II heist thriller entitled *MacTaggart's War* that prestigious publisher Holt Rinehart & Winston released in 1979. It tanked.

He kept writing, but couldn't get anything picked up. In 1982, Pinnacle Books republished *The Charleston Knife is Back In Town*, with an eye towards reviving the series, but abandoned those plans when the reprint sold poorly. Or, as Ralph told author David Everson, because his editor left and the new guy didn't share the previous guy's enthusiasm for the series. Either way, Hardman was dead at Pinnacle ... and soon Pinnacle was, too, locked up the series (and my *.357 Vigilante* books) as assets in their bankruptcy proceedings for another decade.

At the time of his death in 1988, Ralph Dennis was living alone, drinking too much, and working as a clerk at a used book-store in Atlanta. He left behind a suitcase full of unpublished manuscripts.

Although he never achieved the wide audience he deserved during his lifetime, Ralph's books were beloved by crime writers like Bill Crider (who kept shoving the paperbacks into the hands of guys like me) and his close friend Joe R. Lansdale, who generously credited *Hardman* as the inspiration for his wildly success-ful *Hap & Leonard* series.

In April 2012, I finished reading *The Buy Back Blues*, the 12th and final book in the *Hardman* series, and I was heartbroken. I couldn't believe it was the end, that I wouldn't have Jim Hardman and Hump Evans in my life anymore. They weren't just memorable characters in a series of books to me any longer. They'd gotten under my skin, into my blood. I didn't want my relationship with them to be over.

I was addicted.

I'd run out of *Hardmans*, but not books by Ralph Dennis.

I quickly read Ralph's three other published novels. They were good, but they weren't the same as *Hardman*, and in the case of *MacTaggart's War*, what I saw most was the squandered potential, a book that might have succeeded if only he'd had a good editor. It was frustrating…and I wished there was something I could do about it…and some way I could get *Hardman* out to wider audience.

And then it hit me—*maybe I could.*

I'd enjoyed a lot of success self-publishing my out-of-print backlist, in some cases making much more money off the new editions of my books than I did when they were originally released. I figured if I could do it for my own work, why couldn't I do it for Ralph?

I did some digging and learned the rights to Ralph's books had passed to his sister Irma and then, upon her death, to her four heirs. Irma's attorney, Charles Bappert, knew how important it was to his late client that her brother's work would endure and someday reach a wider audience. Charles was kind enough to share with me Ralph's unpublished manuscripts. None of the books was a lost *Hardman*, much to my disappointment, but they had potential if I could do some editorial work on them.

This was how I'd feed my *Hardman* addiction…which, when I got right down to it, was really a deep appreciation for Ralph Dennis' writing and my desire to share it with others.

The next step was making a deal with Ralph's estate. I'd never done anything like that before, so I asked for advice from my friend Joel Goldman, a lawyer-turned-author, on how I should proceed. He'd had a lot of success self-publishing his out-of-print backlist, too, and I knew he was a lot smarter than me. When he learned what I wanted to do, not only did he think it was a good idea, but that it was also a business plan.

A *what?*

A way to make some money, he said. There had to be other books out there, like the *Hardman* series, that never reached the wider audience they deserved ... or perhaps they had, but had fallen out-of-print anyway. Why not use our savvy and experience to bring them back, too?

Sure, why not?

So we launched a publishing company together, Brash Books, and I made my pitch to Ralph's four heirs: I wanted to acquire the copyright to *Hardman* novels, and everything else that Ralph wrote, published and unpublished, and bring them back into print. I wanted the copyright, rather than simply licensing them to republish, so I would have the freedom to make the editorial changes that I felt were necessary to get his unpublished books into shape ... and to significantly revise *MacTaggart's War*.

I needed all four heirs to agree in order to make the deal ... but there was one hold-out who couldn't decide what to do. We were at a standstill.

Meanwhile, Brash Books opened for business in September 2014. We published nearly a hundred titles over the next four years (a mix of reprints and original novels) to critical acclaim and launched an audiobook line. We'd even acquired the copyright to the crime novels by Carolyn Weston, which were the basis for the TV series *The Streets of San Francisco*, and commissioned a successful new book in the series by Robin Burcell.

But it nagged at me that we still didn't have the *Hardman* books that inspired me to invest over $100,000 into launching a publishing company in the first place…just so I could bring them back into print and feed my addiction.

I refused to give up. Twice-a-year, I reached out to Ralph's heirs, hoping the one hold-out would decide to make a deal. In the summer of 2018, it finally happened. I closed the deal. After six long years for me, and decades after the final book in the series was published, Hardman and Hump were coming back.

On December 3, 2018, Brash Books released the first four Hardman novels, with an introduction by Joe R. Lansdale, in trade paperback, ebook and audio editions, and released the remaining eight a few months after that.

The new editions included deeply personal, and often very moving, "afterword" essays by some of Ralph's oldest friends and former students, giving readers a unique perspective on the man and a deeper appreciation of his work. There were also essays by some novelists who love the *Hardman* books and were almost as addicted to them as I am. I say "almost" because I can safely say none of those writers has it quite as bad as me…or would have gone to the lengths I have to feed it. First, I became a publisher and now I've become Ralph Dennis, at least as far as his literary life is concerned.

The reaction among readers and the media to the return of *Hardman* was immediate and enthusiastic…and Hollywood even came calling.

Hardman is mine now.…and so are all of those "lost manuscripts" that Ralph kept in a suitcase. My goal is to get Ralph the wide audience and artistic appreciation that eluded him in his lifetime (and, strangely, he gave me the platform to do it. I would never have become a publisher if not for *Hardman*).

To that end, I cut 35,000 words from *MacTaggart's War* and rearranged the chapters to build character, heighten suspense and tighten the story. It's what an editor should have done for the book back in 1979. Brash released the new edition, retitled *The War Heist*, in March 2019.

I hope to soon begin publishing Ralph's "lost manuscripts." And who knows, maybe someday I'll feed that *Hardman* addiction, and my desire to see those characters again, by writing the 13th book in the series myself.

I just wish that Bill Crider, who passed away in early 2018, was here to see what he started by pushing that book into my hands and getting me hooked.

This is one addiction I'm glad to have…and hope I never shake.

Lee Goldberg is a two-time Edgar & two-time Shamus Award nominee and the #1 *New York Times* bestselling author of over thirty novels, including fifteen *Monk* mysteries, five internationally bestselling Fox & O'Hare books (co-written with Janet Evanovich), and the thrillers *True Fiction, Killer Thriller,* and *Lost Hills.* He's also written and/or produced scores of TV shows, including *Diagnosis Murder, SeaQuest, Nero Wolfe, Baywatch,* and *Monk,* and is the co-creator of the Hallmark mystery movie series *Mystery 101.* As an international television consultant, he has advised networks and studios in Canada, France, Germany, Spain, China, Sweden, and the Netherlands on the creation, writing and production of episodic television series. He is the co-founder, with Joel Goldman, of Brash Books.